T0354636

CONRAD HUESTON

DANCING IN THE REMAINS

iUniverse®

DANCING IN THE REMAINS

This is a work of fiction. All of the characters, names, incidents, organizations, and dialogue in this novel are either the products of the author's imagination or are used fictitiously.

iUniverse books may be ordered through booksellers or by contacting:

iUniverse
1663 Liberty Drive
Bloomington, IN 47403
www.iuniverse.com
1-800-Authors (1-800-288-4677)

ISBN: 978-1-5320-7262-8 (sc)
ISBN: 978-1-5320-7264-2 (hc)
ISBN: 978-1-5320-7263-5 (e)

Library of Congress Control Number: 2019906147

Print information available on the last page.

iUniverse rev. date: 09/06/2019

With special love and thanks to my sister Lauren

I am the empty girl,
The girl with a thousand faces.
But none of them are mine.
I am just a stain,
Driven into the carpet,
Left to fade away.
I'll fade away,
And let others dance in the remains.

—Mindy

PROLOGUE

It was sometime in the late fall. The leaves were old in their color, and life was fading from the dingy green grass. A small vehicle rode past an archaic sign that read Welcome to Gatford. It was a rust bucket of a car. The man who drove it was well aged. The wrinkles on his face were deep, and there was a story in his eyes.

The town was just as he remembered it. The stores had changed, and the town had repaved the roads, but it felt the same. Old men wandered the sidewalks, and young children ran about, both equally directionless.

The old man drove past the town and then down country roads. He weaved his way past cornfields, until he came to an old dirt road. He drove slowly, his wheels thudding in and out of deep potholes. When he came to the end, he parked and walked into the forest. There once had been a trail, but it was long ago overgrown.

After trudging through the thick forest, he broke into a clearing. Long grass swayed as he walked to the skeletal remains of a building that had burned down years ago. The old man still remembered the flames piercing the night. Grass had invaded the building's innards and eaten away at its corpse. An old car not too far away was in a similar state of disarray, more rust than vehicle.

The old man had driven hundreds of miles just to see this. He wasn't sure why. He just felt like he had to. He'd been thinking a lot about his past. About things he wished he could change.

"I'm sorry, my friend." The man's voice was little more than a whisper. "I would have stayed if I'd known what was going to happen."

He stood there for a little while longer. When he left, it was with the realization that no one would set foot there again. The forest would take over the clearing, and the building would be forgotten, along with the memories that were attached to it.

How much life do we choose,
And how much is chosen for us?
Birth is not a choice, and neither is death.
We do not choose our first or last breath,
But the ones in between—
Those are the ones we choose to take.

—Mindy

ONE

Manson walked into the trailer, his face bloody and his knees scraped. Grandma looked up from the newspaper she read.

"Oh dear," she calmly said as she neatly folded her paper. "What did you get up to this time?"

"Fell into a ditch." Manson gazed at the floor, his young eyes frightened of potential scorn.

"Be honest," Grandma said, sternly yet lovingly. "Was it those boys again?"

Manson sniffled, fresh blood dripping from his nose. "They pushed me."

"Did they now?" Grandma pressed a wet rag against Manson's wounds. "I'll have to go have a talk with them."

"No!" Manson pleaded, looking up in earnest. He quickly looked away once Grandma's eyes met his.

"What are you afraid of?"

The blood on Manson's face was gone, absorbed into the moist rag. "They call me a teacher's pet. I don't want them calling me a grandma's boy too."

Grandma wiped clean his bruised knees and rinsed the rag under a stream of hot water. "And what if they do? What will you do?"

"I ... don't know." Tears welled in Manson's eyes.

"Hey," Grandma sweetly said, raising Manson's chin, forcing him to look at her. "Those boys and their words mean nothing. You're smart. They're jealous of that."

"Really?" Manson asked, unsure.

"Yes, really. Now come over here."

They hugged.

"I love you, Grandma."

Grandma took Manson by the shoulders and looked in his eyes. "I love you too."

Manson rode down the street past the railroad tracks. He stopped at the crosswalk, waiting for the light to turn green. His long, greasy blond hair rested on his shoulders as he waited. He rode past the local grocery store, past the elementary and middle schools, past the bus garage, and down country roads. His legs ached, but he didn't care.

He reached the end of a dirt road, which splintered into paths leading deep into the forest. He walked his bike down one of the paths, the sun illuminating him through gaps in the green canopy. The old shack he was accustomed to seeing came into view. Its dingy brown wood looked ready to collapse. A broken window was covered with a sheet, blocking the interior view, but even so, white smoke crept out of the battered frame.

After parking his bike, Manson threw the door wide open. Smoke billowed out, and the sound of coughing could be heard. Manson walked away as the smoke dissipated in the air.

"Tell your friends to leave!" he shouted. He jumped into an old broken-down car that sat next to the building. It was severely rusted, and vines covered its lifeless frame.

"Man ... what the hell?" Dex stumbled out of the shack, a blunt still in his mouth. "Why you gotta ruin the fun, man?"

Manson pulled out a cigarette and lit it. "I told you not to fucking bring anybody out here."

"Remember when you used to be fun?"

Manson blew smoke. "Remember the last time you weren't high?"

Dex chuckled stupidly. "No." Four people stumbled out of the shack. Dex turned to them. "You guys better leave."

Manson tried to ignore the conversation that followed. He closed his eyes and enjoyed his cigarette. Eventually, the voices faded and only Dex was left.

"Somebody's coming to pick them up." He jumped into the passenger's seat.

"Does it look like I give a fuck?"

"Bad day, huh?"

"Every day's a bad day."

"There's your signature optimism!" Dex threw the rest of his blunt out the window. "You know those things kill you, right?" He nodded at the cigarette.

Manson laughed. "You're funny."

"Seriously, man, they'll, like ... destroy your lungs and shit!"

"I've never seen you high enough to take the moral high ground." Manson leaned over and blew smoke in Dex's face. He coughed dramatically.

"How was work?" Dex asked after a little while.

"Same old, same old."

"Fuck Mindy yet?"

"Yeah, we did it on the register in front of all the customers."

Dex shifted lower in his seat. The old cushions moaned beneath him. "Better hit that before it's too late."

"She's seventeen, dude."

"Two years younger than you—big deal. You went to school with her, for fuck's sake!"

Manson knocked ash off the end of his cigarette. It fell through the rusty floor and onto the ground. He took a long drag. Two years? Had it really been that long?

"I'm just sayin', dude, you better bang her before she heads off to college next semester."

"What makes you think she's going to college?"

"Well, she sure as hell ain't stayin' in this shit town. She's too good for that."

"Us, on the other hand ..." Manson said it kiddingly, but on the inside, it sat like a blister.

"Maybe you, man. I'm outta here soon."

"Yeah, where?" Manson asked in mocking disbelief.

"Colorado. Gonna live with my cousin."

Manson snapped his head toward Dex. "Are you serious right now?"

"Yeah, I'm leavin' at the end of the summer." Dex sank even lower in his seat until he was practically lying down. "My cousin's got me set up with a job and everything. And in Colorado, I can smoke all the kush I want. Better than kush, there's men!"

Manson was silent. He let the rest of his cigarette fall to the floor, got out of the car, and left.

Dex didn't notice. He kept talking, until he suddenly realized he was alone. When he looked up, he saw Manson walking his bike to the road and shouted after him, "Did you bring any munchies!"

"They're by the shack, where my bike was parked."

"I love you!"

"You're a homo."

"Always and forever."

Manson rode back slower than he'd come. The wheels turned methodically against the pavement. He didn't want to go home. He couldn't remember the last time he did.

He rode through the trailer park, slower and slower, until he came to his house. It was small, cramped, and ugly. He walked inside. As always, the curtains were drawn. His mom was sitting in front of the TV, smoking a cigarette. Her eyes were baggy, and her movements were slow.

"How was work?" Her voice was coarse.

"Fine."

"You should go see Grandma. She's been asking for you all day."

"No, she hasn't," Manson said resentfully. "She's been asking for Dan." His mother didn't look away from the TV. Manson marched to the back room, gently tapping on the door.

"Dan, is that you?"

"Sure is, Grandma." Manson walked in gently, closing the door behind him. The room was stuffy, and it smelled.

"I heard you're in the military!"

"Sure am, Grandma." Manson sat on the bed next to her. She was propped up against the backboard.

"Are you enjoying it?"

Manson gave the same answer he always did. He'd had this conversation too many times to count.

"How's your brother doing?"

5

The conversation always came to this question. Usually near the end. It was the part that Manson hated the most.

"Manson's fine." He couldn't find it in him to say anything else.

"Did he graduate?"

"Yes."

"Oh good! We were worried there for a while that he wouldn't make it!"

"You shouldn't worry about him so much, Grandma. He's an A student," Manson said through gritted teeth and watery eyes.

"I love him and all, but he doesn't have the drive you have! And his friend Dex? A bad influence, that boy is! He does illegal drugs and has intercourse with men! Ever since ..."

Manson listened to the spiel drag on and on. He looked at his grandma's withered face. She didn't have much longer; he knew this. He only had to endure this living hell for a little while longer. The all-too-familiar guilt hit him as he fantasized about her death. Eventually, she fell asleep. He snuck out and went into his room, where he lay on the bed, gazing numbly at the ceiling. His grandma's words echoed in his head, and he felt like dying.

Life looks so small from a distance.
Everything looks better in remembrance.
Except love.
Love is always better in the present.
You can cherish each kiss, every touch,
His fingers around your waist.
You can taste
His saliva and feel his warmth.
When you're that close to another human,
Life seems huge.

—Mindy

TWO

It was usually dark before Manson made it home. It was a habit he'd formed as soon as he was given the freedom. He cycled up to the small porch and tied his bike to the railing. Dan sat outside, smoking a fat cigar.

"What happened to good old cigarettes?" Manson asked as he walked up to Dan.

Dan puffed. "Cigars are better."

"More … militaristic?" Manson smiled.

"I guess you could say that." Dan smiled as Manson sat down next to him. "I see your eyes are red again."

Manson shrugged. "Dex always has some."

"Just make sure your grades stay up."

"You don't have to worry about that. School is easy."

"Mmm," Dan commented blandly. "I'll be calling to make sure you stay on top of that shit."

"Are you excited?" Manson asked as he rested his hands behind his head. "You're finally doing it."

"It's exciting," Dan said with a sigh. "And scary."

Manson looked at his brother. "Scary?"

"Of course," Dan admitted. "All I've ever known is this shit town. Tomorrow, I'm off to boot camp, and after that ... a whole new country."

Manson looked up at the starry sky. "No matter where you are, we'll both be looking at the same sky."

"That's some gay shit," Dan remarked.

"Fuck off."

They both laughed.

"I love you," Dan said after some silence.

Manson smiled. "And I'm the gay one?"

"Seriously, I'll miss you." Dan puffed on his cigar. "This whole time ... it's been us against the world."

"It still is," Manson said. "That won't change." He looked at the cigar hanging from Dan's lips. "Can I try it?"

"Sure." Dan handed the stogie over. "You puff it. You don't inhale."

"Tastes like ass," Manson said as he handed it back. "And not a good ass."

Dan laughed. "To each his own, I suppose."

"I guess." Manson stood up. "I'm going to bed. And Dan?" Dan looked over his shoulder as his brother walked inside. "I love you too."

Gunfire. Sand jumped around Dan's feet as bullets whizzed by. The desert sprawled before him, a seemingly never-ending abyss. His friends and fellow soldiers ran on either side. Their boots trudged through the sand, every grain holding them back from the life they so desperately clung to.

A land mine went off. Dan didn't have time to care. He only had time to run. The explosion left his ears ringing. He passively realized that he was covered in someone else's blood.

Another land mine. And another. Someone had been shot. Dan saw the man fall in his periphery. The man screamed. Soon it was just Dan. Endless desert sprawled before him as death rode his back. Then a bullet entered the back of his head. This was how he died.

"Sir?"

Dan awoke in a cold sweat. He was in his bunk. Alive.

"Sir, there's an emergency call for you. There's been a death in the family." The soldier averted his eyes. "I'm sorry for your loss, sir."

The next morning Manson was glad to leave. He didn't like work all that much, but it was better than being at home. The stale, stuffy air was oppressive and smelled of slow death. He threw on his uniform and marched out the door. His mom was already up, sitting where she always sat. She tried to say goodbye, but he was out the door before she could mutter a word. She looked blankly at the door and took a drag from her cigarette. Her eyes wandered back to the TV.

The gas station was only a few blocks from Manson's house. It sat on the only major road that ran through the small town of Gatford. Manson tied up his bike behind the building, next to the dumpsters, and walked in.

He would never admit it to himself, but the best part of his day was seeing Mindy. She was average-looking but cute, with brown eyes and a bright smile. She looked at him as he walked in.

"I was wondering when you were going to show up." Her long ringlets were expertly braided to her head.

"I'm ten minutes early!" Manson said as he stepped behind the counter. His eyes fluttered down to Mindy's wrists. He quickly looked away. He didn't want her knowing he was looking at her scars.

"You're usually *fifteen* minutes early."

"Do you keep track of all my habits?"

Mindy shrugged.

The gas station was small, with only two aisles for customers. "It's pretty slow today," Manson said blandly.

"Eh." Mindy chewed a piece of gum. "I'm sure we'll get a rush sooner or later."

Manson looked Mindy up and down when she wasn't looking. They joked and bantered, but Manson barely knew her. He wanted to, though. He wanted to ask her questions, take her on a date, get to know her … but something stopped him. Something always stopped him.

The day dragged on, as usual. Customers came and went. Manson took a smoke break, and Mindy ate lunch. They chatted with the same people who came in every day. Manson was so used to the routine that it almost felt robotic.

When it came time to leave, Manson stood out back, having his last smoke of the workday. He lazily watched clouds dance in front of a bright orange sky. Cars whizzed by noisily, passing archaic buildings and run-down shops. Manson looked down at his feet, dragging them pointlessly across the hot pavement.

"Still hangin' around?"

Manson looked up as Mindy walked around the corner. Her arms were crossed, and she wore a playful smile.

"I thought you left." Smoke cascaded out of Manson's lips as he talked.

"Naw, I decided to hang back and stalk you." She playfully nudged him with her shoulder.

Butterflies danced in his stomach, but feeling stupid, he quickly silenced them. "Just what I need—a stalker." He tried to be cool but came off as aggressive.

"All right, Mr. Grumpy," Mindy said, walking away. "Guess I shouldn't have interrupted your alone time."

"No, wait!" The words slipped out of his mouth before he realized it. Mindy spun around. He desperately looked for something to follow up but found only silence.

"Yeah?" Mindy asked impatiently.

"What are you doing tonight?"

"Nothing." A sly smile spread across her face. "You want to do something?"

"Sure." Manson tried to act nonchalant, but Mindy just chuckled.

"How about you show me where you go every night after work."

"What?"

"Your house is that way." She pointed toward the trailer park. "But you always bike that way." She pointed down the street.

"Wow, you really are my stalker." Manson had regained some of his cool. He threw the rest of his cigarette on the ground. "I'm not sure if we can both fit on my bike."

"We can try."

Manson got on first, scooting to the very front of the seat. Mindy jumped on behind him, wrapping her arms around his stomach and resting her chin on his shoulder. Warm blood coursed through Manson, but he forced himself to calm down. They biked slowly out of the parking lot and down the street.

"You wanna tell me where we're going?" Mindy asked as they rode over the railroad tracks.

"Well ... we're not going where I usually go." Manson hopped off, and Mindy followed.

"Why?"

The truth was, he didn't want to introduce her to Dex. He'd rather be alone. But he chose a simpler answer. "I have something better to show you."

Manson tied his bike to a tree, and they headed down the railroad tracks. Their heels scraped against wood and ridged rocks. There were steep hills on either side of the tracks and forest beyond that. A light breeze sent the wind into motion as well as Mindy's braid. She reached up to untie it, letting her long natural curls bounce about. She threw both of her arms out, closed her eyes, and tipped her head back.

"What are you doing?" Manson asked with a smile.

"Enjoying the fresh air." She opened her eyes and jumped onto one of the beams. "Give me your hand."

Manson reached up, grabbing Mindy as she balanced. Their fingers intertwined. A giddy feeling went through him. He held her there for a while, her feet wobbly against the metal.

"I give up," she said, falling gently down onto the tracks. "I was never good at that."

Manson noticed that they were still holding hands. "Do ... do you want me to let go?" His voice was a whisper.

"Only if you want to."

He didn't want to.

After walking for a while, Manson led Mindy off the beaten path and into the forest. He held her hand tightly and guided her through the dense forest along an old path.

"I feel like you're leading me nowhere," Mindy said, long grass cutting at her heels.

"Me and my brother used to come here all the time," Manson said.

"You have a brother?"

"Yeah." Manson didn't bother to elaborate.

They broke through dense underbrush, and Mindy gasped in amazement. They were standing on a ledge that plummeted down toward a thick mass of rocks. Beyond that, she could see the entire forest; a small stream ran through its center. Gatford sat beyond the greenery, its buildings looking like insignificant dots. The scenery was illuminated by the pink sky and the orange glow of the setting sun.

"There's the gas station!" Mindy said, pointing. "Life looks so small from a distance." She settled onto the ground, sitting cross-legged. Manson did the same, leaning his back against a tree. Mindy scooted over to him, laying her head on his chest. He tried to quiet the pounding of his heart, but he knew she could hear.

"You come here often?" Mindy asked.

"Used to. When I was a kid."

"Why'd you stop?"

Manson shrugged. "Grew up. Life got in the way."

"That's always a mistake. Growing up." Mindy slid down until her head was resting on Manson's thigh. Her body was sprawled across the grass, her dark skin illuminated by the evening sky. Her sundress blew in the warm breeze, but she didn't seem to mind.

"Why did you bring me here?"

"I thought it would be romantic." Manson's heart skipped a beat. He hadn't expected to answer so honestly.

Mindy tipped her head back, resting her chin on Manson's leg. "And now your true intentions come to light!" She smiled widely.

Manson blushed, despite himself.

"Well, if this is a date, then let's play twenty questions." Mindy sat up, resting on her haunches.

"Twenty questions?"

Mindy gasped in mock horror. "You've never played twenty questions? It's really simple. We ask each other questions until we've both asked twenty questions."

"Sounds simple. You go first."

"Have you ever had sex?" She said it quickly and without hesitation.

Manson's eyes widened. "That's kinda ... personal."

"That's the point of the game." Mindy leaned backward, propping herself up with her elbows. Strands of hair fell across her face.

"I did a few times in high school," Manson answered, rubbing the back of his head nervously.

"With who?"

"You only get one question at a time!" Manson blurted. "Those are the rules, right?"

Mindy rolled her eyes playfully. "Go ahead. Your turn."

Manson sighed, glad to change the topic. "What are your future plans?"

"Oh, come on!" Mindy exclaimed. "That's such a generic question!" She sat up, her arms dirty from resting on the ground. "My immediate future or the distant future?"

"Both."

Mindy sighed. "Well, I know what's about to happen in my immediate future." She stood up over Manson and then sat down on his lap, her legs wrapping around his waist. Manson looked into her eyes as his heart raced.

"I have a question." She wrapped her arms around his head. "Why haven't you kissed me yet?"

Manson leaned in.

They didn't reach twenty questions.

By the time they started walking back, it was dark. They stumbled blindly down the railroad tracks, hand in hand. Manson rode his bike slowly across the cool pavement. He didn't want the night to end. Mindy's cheek was resting against his upper back, and her hands were wrapped around him. When they reached the gas station, Manson said what he'd been thinking.

"I don't want this to end."

Mindy hopped off. "It doesn't have to." She leaned in for one last, lingering kiss. "Same time tomorrow?"

"Yeah …" Manson said dreamily.

"Good."

Manson watched as she walked away.

But that date never happened. When Manson got home his fairy-tale day came to a crashing end. When he walked in, his mom wasn't sitting in her usual place. The door to his grandma's room was open, and he could hear soft weeping. He walked in to see an empty bed.

INTERLUDE

The first time I cut myself was in the seventh grade. I sat in the bath and used a pair of scissors I'd stolen from school. I did it on my thigh so no one could see. The blood seeped from the wound and into the water like a red ghost emerging from its fleshy cave. It floated up, looking somehow gorgeous. I only let the bathwater escape down the drain when the whole thing had a tint of red in its blue complexion.

I only started cutting my wrists when the empty chasm inside me had grown to such depths that I did not care if the world knew it was there. Besides, I had no more room on my thighs for new scars. I remember the cool blood running from my wrists and down my palm. It invaded the creases of my skin and dripped off the edge of my fingertips into the sink. That's when my mom walked in.

"What are you doing!" I'd never heard her scream like that.

"Dying," I said, not seeing the problem.

What's so strange about wanting to die? We all do it at some point; why delay the inevitable? *There I go again, with my insanity.* The stray thoughts moving in and out of my mind were like refuse moving with the tide—a tide I wish I could jump into. To be pulled into the waves and dance with them. And when the dead corpse of a girl washes up on shore, make sure to bury her with her words.

—Mindy
(Journal Entry)

Dreams and nightmares are the same.
They are the deep secrets that lie in your brain.
And once you learn the meaning,
You will never be the same.

—Mindy

THREE

The first day of high school was over. Manson rode side by side with Dex, as they lazily pedaled along the warm concrete.

"Dude, is it just me, or did Amber get a lot hotter over the summer?"

"Yeah, I guess so." Dex looked uncomfortable. "Dude … can I tell you something?"

"Sure."

"I don't think I'm into chicks."

"What are you into then? Fucking pine cones?"

"Dude, I think I'm into dudes."

"Nice, dude." Manson raised one hand to shield his eyes from the sun, the other remaining on the handlebar. "You like those fat cocks?" He laughed.

Dex looked annoyed. "I'm serious, dude."

"I know." Manson did a small jump, his wheels bouncing on the concrete. "I don't really care, dude. You could be into shoving doorknobs up your ass, and I wouldn't give a shit."

"That's probably the nicest thing you've ever said to me."

"Which part? The doorknob part or the I-don't-give-a-shit part?"

"All of it."

The two continued riding, the sun laying into their backs.

Manson took the next week off work. He didn't really want to, but he felt like it was the right thing to do. He was supposed to be grieving. In actuality, all he felt was guilt. Guilt that he wasn't grieving. He wasn't happy his grandma was gone, but he wasn't sad either. He just felt numb. He kept flashing back to the nights he'd spent with her.

Dan was flying in for the funeral. Manson tried not thinking about that. He'd deal with his brother when he arrived. He spent his week off with Dex, smoking weed in the shack. The inside of the shack was pimped out with posters and various weed-related decorations. Random cushions were strewn on the floor, and a hammock hung from the exposed roof beams. Manson sat on a beat-up green couch in the corner.

He'd occasionally go home to check on his mom, but he couldn't handle her grief. He had held her while she cried on his grandma's bed. He couldn't do it again. His nights were spent in the shack, wrapping himself in cushions and lying on the couch. Sometimes Dex would stay with him.

"You wanna talk about it, dude?"

"No," Manson said simply.

The shack became clouded with smoke, as did Manson's mind. He looked blankly through the fog, taking one hit after another. He was afraid to stop. He was afraid of being sober. He was afraid of going back home. Maybe his grandma would still be there, asking for Dan.

On the fifth day, Dex dragged him back home. "You've had enough." He opened the door and let the shack air out. "You know that it's true if I'm saying it!" Dex's levity did not cheer Manson up.

Manson's feet dragged as Dex walked him back to town. They passed the railroad tracks and the gas station. Manson's mind wandered to Mindy for a moment. He saw her vividly, but when she opened her mouth, his grandma spoke. "Dan ..."

Dex opened the front door without knocking. Manson's mom was back to her usual position in front of the TV. "Hey, Dex," she said blankly.

"Hey. Manson's a little out of it, so I walked him home."

Later that night, Manson lay on his bed, with Dex sitting beside him. The fog in Manson's mind was clearing. "I feel better, dude," he said, staring at the ceiling. "You can go home if you want."

"You sure? I can spend the night."

"No, dude, it's fine. I'm going to go back to work in the morning."

"If you need anything, just call. I'm here for ya, dude." Dex walked out, leaving Manson alone.

Manson had a dream that night. His feet lightly tread over soft wood tracks, like feathers floating through the air. The tracks wove through a field of bright green grass. The sun was high in the sky, shining so brightly that it seemed to cast a fog of light.

Manson was almost gliding toward a distant tree line. He heard a train in the distance. As he got closer, he saw a figure standing on the tracks. It was Mindy. Her back was to him.

The train was louder now. Manson's feet got heavier as he kept walking. The sun was going down quickly, as if it were in sync with his footsteps. Mindy wore a bright sundress that blew

25

in a breeze that was getting progressively harsher. Soon it was a whirlwind, so strong Manson felt as if he might be blown away.

"Mindy!" he shouted. "Mindy!"

He felt panic. Something was wrong. She was in danger. The train whistle blew louder than before. Manson could see billowing smoke coming from within the forest. He ran, but his legs were like bricks, dragging him across the harsh wood tracks. He was getting close to her now. The sun had disappeared into the trees. The train was no longer a distant noise. Manson could see it. Its bright light shone like a spark, but the spark was quickly growing into a flame. He could hear the turning of the wheels like the bellowing screams of a vicious monster.

"Mindy!" Manson was only a few steps away now. Darkness had taken over the landscape; the only light was from the fast-approaching train. Mindy was a black silhouette, staring at oncoming death. Bright light cascaded around her, casting shadows onto the surrounding forest. The branches waved in the wind, like fingers aimlessly reaching.

"Mindy!" Manson reached out his hand, grabbing her shoulder. The train was on top of them now, moments away from running them down. Manson spun Mindy around, looking into her eyes before they both died. Except they weren't her eyes. They were his grandma's. Manson suddenly noticed the noose around her neck.

"Dan."

The name cut through him like a knife. The train whistle blew, the wheels chugged on, and the light overtook Manson's vision. He woke up, sweaty and alone, the sound of the train still echoing in his head.

Popping pills,
Until your stomach is filled
With happiness. Changing the chemistry
Of the brain until you are no longer the same
Person. Some are addicted to religion,
And others are addicted to the delusion of decision.
We all have our own self-made prescriptions,
But in the end, we only have one decision:
Life or death.

—Mindy

FOUR

Dan played on the living room floor. His fat toddler fingers moved army men about in a sporadic formation. Their little green heads had teeth marks—that is, those that weren't fully decapitated. Mother sat not far away, looking blankly out the window. She nervously twiddled her fingers, the way someone did if they were getting ready to release a secret.

"Mom …"

Grandma was in the kitchen, her fingers pruney from doing dishes. "What is it, hon?"

Mom looked down at the floor. "There's something …" She bit her lip. "I'm … I'm pregnant."

Grandma froze, dropping the plate she'd been washing. It plopped into the sink and floated slowly to the bottom. "What?"

"I'm pregnant. Again."

There was a long silence.

"Do you know who the father is?"

"No."

"Jesus Christ." Grandma rubbed her temples, forgetting her hands were wet. Another long silence. "We can't afford this."

"Do you only think about money?" Mom looked at Dan, a teary gleam growing in her eye.

"One of us has to!" Grandma exclaimed. "My Social Security barely pays for this house!"

"I'll get a second job."

Grandma scoffed. "You'll be lucky if you can keep the one you have."

That's when the arguing began. The endless arguing. Dan played with army men, oblivious to the conflict.

Mindy eagerly awaited Manson, but he never came in for work. She was angry with him at first—they had a date that night! How could he skip out? Then she heard the news. Her stomach sank like a stone being thrown into the ocean. Deeper and deeper it sank until it hit a black abyss.

When she drove home that night, she felt numb. She flashbacked to the night before. She saw the forest below her as she rested her head against Manson. That was the happiest she had felt in a long time. It only made sense that it would end like this.

The familiar numbness stayed with her as she walked into her apartment. She stood in the entryway, a long hallway stretching out before her. She heard her mom in the kitchen, making dinner. She smelled the familiar scent of spaghetti and meatballs. Her little brother was in front of the TV, the blue light bathing his wide eyes. She heard her dad on the phone. Probably talking to someone from work. She wanted to stay in that moment. Hearing and seeing but not being a part of the world around her.

"Honey!" her mom exclaimed. "Is that you?"

Her solidarity was broken. "Who else?"

"Can you help me with dinner? *Thomas*, you're sitting too close to the TV!"

Mindy helped with dinner. She dragged her body around and smiled when she was supposed to, talked when it made sense, and lied and said her day had been good. She even played video games with her brother after they ate. It's what a good sister would have done.

"Don't forget to take your pills!" Mindy's mom shouted as her daughter walked into the bathroom. Mindy took a hot shower, letting the water run down her torso and burn her skin. She stood there until the water ran cold.

She pulled the curtain back and dried herself off. She stared into the mirror, gazing blankly at the cuts on her wrists. Her eyes wandered to a small container sitting at the edge of the sink. She grabbed it and took out a small red pill. It sat in her palm as she contemplated.

Take it. It'll make you better.

Something inside wouldn't let her.

She dumped it into the toilet and flushed.

Manson came back today. Mindy kept reminding herself of this. She wore a tight shirt and revealing jeans. She felt stupid. His grandma had just died. He wouldn't care what she was wearing.

She kept one eye on the door as she dealt with customers. What would she say to him? *Sorry your grandma died. Wanna go on a date again?* She was selfish for thinking that, but she couldn't help it. Her mind kept flashing back to the night on the cliff. All she could think about was having another night like that.

When Manson showed up, he stumbled in late. His eyes were bloodshot, and his hair was a tangled mess. He blundered forward as if in a stupor.

31

"Hey," Mindy said quietly.

Manson lazily joined her behind the counter. His eyes were downcast. "Hey." His voice was a crackly whisper.

The store was empty; the only sound was the hum of the air conditioner. Mindy wished customers would walk in and distract her from the awkward silence. She searched desperately for something to say.

"Are you ... all right?"

"No."

The honesty of Manson's answer caught Mindy off guard. A prolonged silence followed that seemed to stretch into infinity.

"Would you ..." Manson said, "would you wanna talk? After work?"

"Yes." Mindy said it a little too eagerly.

A customer suddenly walked in and loudly stomped down the aisles. Manson's eyes drifted off into the distance, and Mindy stared at him. They didn't talk much during work. There was nothing else they could say.

"Are we going back into the forest?" Mindy was on the back of Manson's bike, her arms once again wrapped around him.

"No." Manson's long legs swung methodically with the rhythm of the pedals. They were heading into the center of town. The cracked streets were full of potholes, and the sidewalk was infested with patches of grass. Children rode on scooters, yelling at each other. The occasional adult cut through them, their grown-up frowns bringing the children to silence.

Manson pulled into a desolate parking lot. A run-down strip mall ran parallel to them. Half the shops were vacant, and the ones that weren't were largely empty. Manson led Mindy into a shop with a big rusty sign that read MIKE'S MIGHTY SUBS.

"Why did you bring me here?" Mindy stood behind Manson, holding his hand tightly.

"My friend works here, so I get discounts."

Perplexed, Mindy looked up at Manson. "I thought you wanted to talk."

"We will."

The restaurant was large, but only a few customers sat at the sporadically placed tables. Old men who had been going there for years chomped down on subs they'd ordered a million times over. There was a counter at the back, and behind that, a kitchen. At one time it might have been bustling with multiple chefs, shouting orders at each other. Now, it slumped forward lethargically, like a heart that was slowly losing its beat.

"What do you want?" Manson asked as they walked toward the counter.

"Um ... whatever you're having." Mindy was trying to figure out what was going through Manson's head. *Is this how grieving people act? Is this what grieving people do? Go on dates?*

Dex looked at Manson in surprise as he approached the counter. He wore a bland black uniform that was covered in flour and a hat that read *Mike's Mighty Subs.* "Hey, dude," he said cautiously. "How are you doing?" The question was more than a formality.

"I'm doing better."

"You must be Mindy." Dex followed the trail from Manson's arm to Mindy's hand. "I'm Dex." He smiled.

"Hi." She smiled back.

"You wanna Philly-style sub, right?" Dex asked Manson.

"Make it two."

A little while later, they sat at the back of the restaurant in a grimy-looking booth next to a large window that looked onto the parking lot. Manson scarfed down his sandwich. Mindy barely touched hers. She was beginning to realize this was a bad idea.

"Listen …" she said, trying to state her thoughts in the most delicate way possible. "I think I should go. You seem to still be … grieving."

"But I'm not." Manson set down his sub. "This week has been one of the best of my life."

Mindy was startled. "Are you sure you're okay?"

"I never said I was okay." He leaned back in his seat, his eyes looking past Mindy and out the window. "Can I ask you something?" Mindy didn't have time to answer before he continued. "What are your plans for the future?"

"You asked this last time we—"

"You never answered." Manson's eyes shot toward her.

He looked deranged. If Mindy didn't know better, she'd have been scared.

"Well … I'm going to college."

"What about after that?"

"Get a job?" Mindy shrugged. "What does this have to do with any—"

"You see?" Manson leaned forward, ignoring her. His index finger waved around in the air as he made his point. "We all have these plans. They all follow the same basic formula. Go to school, get a job, get married, have kids …" He leaned back again, his legs spread wide and his feet twitching. "Nobody talks about what's after that, though. Nobody talks about death."

There was silence as Mindy contemplated whether or not to press on with the conversation. She didn't want to antagonize a grieving man. Her desire to understand Manson's grief trumped her better senses.

"Have you looked around this town?" Mindy smiled in a sad sort of way. "There's a church on every street corner. All people do here is prepare for death."

"No," Manson said. "They prepare for more life because they're scared of death. They're scared of it ending so they say it continues. Nobody actually plans on dying. People don't say, 'I'm going to grow up, get a job, and die!'" Manson slammed his finger against the table with every point he made. "Death comes for all of us, yet it doesn't work into our plans. Instead, we plan distractions."

"You said this week was the best of your life?" The statement was a question.

Manson sighed. His bombastic mannerisms stopped. An abrupt calm suddenly enveloped him. "I never had the chance to make plans." Manson was looking at something that wasn't there. "When my brother left ... I had to step up. I had to start paying the bills. My mom's unemployment wasn't cutting it. I had to take care of my grandma. Every night I talked to her, and every night she called me by my brother's name. In this last week ... I wasn't called Dan once."

Mindy was overcome with emotion. She felt her eyes growing moist and her throat clenching shut. She now understood this man's grief. She leaned forward and kissed him. His lips were still greasy from the sub.

I find solace in his kiss.
Even if we haven't spoken the words,
I know he understands my sorrow.
I can feel it in his touch,
In the sudden rush
Of his fingertips brushing
My torso. There is so much
That can be explained in a single touch.

—Mindy

FIVE

"Why don't you go after her, dude?"

"I don't know, man … I don't think she'd go for a guy like me."

Manson's back was pressed against one of the school's white brick walls. Students and teachers alike bustled about. Manson's eyes stayed steady on a freshman girl. Mindy.

"You're an upperclassman, dude." Dex rubbed his red eyes. "That, like, gives you an advantage."

"I don't know." Despite Manson's casual attitude, his eyes stayed glued on Mindy. "I always thought it was creepy when upperclassmen went after freshmen girls."

"You're worried about your dick being too small, arnt ya?"

"Fuck off, dude." Manson looked away, his eyes focusing on the white tile floor.

"It's okay, dude; the idea that girls prefer big dicks is a myth." Dex rubbed his eyes again. "All genitalia are created equal. It's all about what you do with it not—" Dex looked around, suddenly aware he was alone. He caught a glimpse of Manson's back as he disappeared into the crowd. "Come on, man!" Dex walked after him. "I was just fucking with you! Don't be angry because I said you have a small dick."

They rode around the town for a bit, neither of them really wanting to part ways. Mindy gazed at the town as it passed by. Sadness overtook her. It seemed to reflect from the streets and onto her soul. She sucked on her bottom lip, the wet grease of Manson's kiss falling onto her tongue. The warmness of his back pressed itself into her cheek.

Mindy suddenly realized she didn't know how to define her relationship with Manson. What were they? They were stuck in a strange place, somewhere between a budding relationship and the grief of a death. She decided not to care. Whatever they were, at least they *were*.

"Do you want me to drop you off at your car?" Manson asked.

"I don't know." Mindy tightened her arms around his stomach. Manson heard what was not said and kept riding. There was an unacknowledged need for each other's company. He drove her to the shack. He took the bike as far into the forest as he could before they had to walk.

"This is amazing!" Mindy exclaimed as they walked into the small building. Mindy's eyes floated from the makeshift hammock that hung above her to the posters and decorations that popped off the walls.

"It's not much," Manson said nonchalantly. "Just the place Dex and I come to smoke and drink."

Mindy plopped down onto the old couch, the springs fighting back against her weight. She spread herself out, leaning her head against the grimy cushions. "This smells like cat piss."

"Don't blame us." Manson sat down beside her. "We picked it up off the side of the road."

"That explains it." She turned her head toward Manson, her cheekbones highlighted by her smile. "Want to play twenty questions?"

"Again?"

"We never finished our last game."

"We may not even start this one." He smiled and leaned in, but Mindy put a finger to his lips.

"Down boy," she commanded slyly.

Manson sat back with a sigh. "Okay ... you go first."

"What's your deepest fear?" Mindy tucked her legs under her and sat up on her knees. She gazed lovingly at Manson as his eyes wandered, as if looking for an appropriate answer.

"You always have the funniest questions."

Mindy smiled at Manson's sarcasm. "I try."

"My deepest fear ..." Manson began cautiously, "would be living in this town until I die. Being trapped here for my entire life."

"What's wrong with here?"

"Everything," Manson said bitterly.

"*I'm* here." Mindy feigned offense.

"That's the one good thing." He leaned in, but once again Mindy's finger touched his lips.

"Why don't you leave?" Mindy let her finger sit there. "You're old enough to move out."

"It's not that simple. I have to take care of my ..." Manson paused, realizing his mistake.

"Grandma?" Mindy sadly stated.

There was an awkward silence before Manson steered the conversation in another direction. "My question, right?"

Mindy nodded.

"Do you have any hobbies?"

"Your questions are so lame." Mindy rolled her eyes playfully. "I write."

"Write what?"

"Poems, short stories …" Mindy's eyes glazed over as her mind wandered to subjects she was unwilling to share.

Manson leaned forward, trying to look her in the eye. "Hello … Earth to Mindy?"

"Sorry." She shook the thoughts out of her head. "I write all kinds of stuff." She reached into her back pocket and pulled out a small, crumpled notebook. "Journals … I tried a book once, but I don't have the attention span to stick with it."

"Can I read some of it?"

"Of course." Mindy's voice lacked confidence.

"If you don't want me to, that's fine."

"It's not that. It's just …" Mindy shifted as she searched for the words. "Sharing my work is hard. I put so much time and thought into it, and it feels like when people read it, it doesn't impact them in the way I want it to. It doesn't impact people in the same way it does me."

"I get that," Manson said. "When you make something, it matters to you on a deep level."

Mindy doubted he understood. "If you want to read some, you can."

Manson opened the messy notepad. Loose pieces of paper dangled from flimsy paper clips. Messy cursive outlined the pages. The occasional sketch broke the monotony of words. Manson flipped through, transfixed. "This is amazing."

"You haven't read anything yet."

"I know, but it's still amazing."

He abruptly stopped at a page with the word *sorrow* written at the top. It was less cluttered than the other passages. There was a small sketch of a girl shrouded in darkness. Her long hair and colorless eyes were the only things visible. Underneath the shadowy figure, there was a poem.

Sorrow is a word that shouldn't be,
Because what it expresses can only be felt, not explained.
To try to explain an emotion in a single word is heresy.
Love, joy … these are profound concepts.
Emotions should be expressed with novels the size of Bibles,
Not with single words.
For what is sorrow
But a word?

Mindy winced. "Why did you have to choose that one? It's so bad."

"No," Manson's said, "it's amazing."

Mindy gazed at Manson as he continued to flip through the notebook. She felt the overwhelming need to kiss him. She leaned in and, unlike her, he was not the kind to turn down the offer.

They say blood runs thicker than water,
But water keeps me alive,
And I only see blood when I hurt.
They say blood runs thicker than water,
But they've never seen a river from their wrists,
Falling from their skin and onto their sheets.
They say blood runs thicker than water,
But what do they know?
Only what they've been told.

—Mindy

SIX

"Hey, could you give me a ride to Dex's house?"

Manson stopped his brother as he walked onto the porch. Dan had a cigarette hanging from his mouth and his football gear on.

"Why can't you ride your bike?" Smoke wafted out of Dan's mouth as he talked. He clutched his football helmet under his arm.

"My tire popped. It's at Dex's house. He's going to help me fix it."

Dan looked down at his watch. "I got time. Hop in."

Dan's beat-down rust bucket spewed fumes as they backed out of the driveway. The windows were rolled down. Manson gazed at the town passing by while his brother inhaled smoke.

"So I heard Dex came out."

"Yeah," Manson responded blankly.

"How long have you known?"

"About a year."

"You guys aren't …?"

"Fuck off. I'm not gay."

"Just checking." Dan threw his cigarette butt out the window. It bounced against the concrete, smoldering into oblivion. "You could tell me if you were."

"I'm not fucking gay."

"You seem to be getting mighty defensive." Dan smiled, going from genuine concern to playful jesting. Manson ignored him.

"Can I have some of your cigarettes?"

"No."

"Why?"

"You know why." Unconsciously, Dan reached for another smoke. "Grandma found your stash the other day. If she knows I'm the one who's been giving them to you, I'll be screwed."

"She won't know if you give me one."

Dan came to a slow stop at an intersection. He didn't say anything as he looked both ways before continuing.

Manson dropped the subject as he watched the houses pass by. "I saw you talking to the recruiter in the cafeteria the other day. Have you chosen a branch yet?"

"Not yet." Dan lit the cigarette he'd been clutching between his fingers. "I'm thinking of the army. Have you been looking into colleges?"

"Not yet. I have almost three years."

"You need to get on that shit now." Dan passed his brother the lit cigarette, letting him take a drag. "Your grades are so good you could get a full ride at the right college."

"Yeah." Manson's voice was wheezy as smoke suppressed his breath.

Dan came to a stop. They were on the outskirts of town. Dex's house was run-down, and his lawn was unkempt. Manson began to step out, but Dan stopped him.

"Here." He handed Manson the rest of his pack of smokes. "Don't bring them back home. I won't get in trouble because of your bitch ass."

In the week leading up to Dan's return, Manson's mother came back to life. She no longer sat endlessly in front of the TV. She scurried around the house, trying to accomplish an endless list of chores. She pulled the curtains back, illuminating the house. She opened the windows, airing out the smell of cigarette smoke and stale air. She decorated with flowers and pulled her hair back, revealing a vibrancy that hadn't been there since her youth.

Manson smoked a lot of cigarettes leading up to Dan's return. At one point, he went through two packs a day. The taste on his tongue described how he felt.

When the day finally came, Manson desperately avoided the inevitable. He didn't go home after work. Instead, he went to the shack with Mindy. Dex was already there, sitting shirtless in a lawn chair. Mindy and Manson sat in the old car, watching the summer leaves shimmer in front of an obscured sun. Manson puffed on a cigarette, exhaling smoke out his nose. Mindy leaned against his arm, lovingly. The smoke cascaded toward her, brushing her cheek like the misty white finger of a ghost. She brushed up against Manson like a cat slinking by someone's leg.

Manson looked at her. She was so beautiful. Everything about her was perfect, from her wide, sculpted cheeks to her curvy torso to her smooth, dark-brown skin. He still couldn't believe she wanted him.

"My brother comes back today," Manson blurted.

"Back from the military, right?"

"Yeah."

"He's visiting, then?"

"He came back for the funeral." Manson said it in a way that made Mindy look at him with concern.

She sat up, the scars on her wrist rubbing against his arm. "Are you doing okay?"

"I guess so."

"Want to talk about it?"

"There's not much to talk about."

Manson could feel Mindy's eyes pressing into him. She leaned over and kissed him on the cheek. Manson's troubles were forgotten as butterflies danced in his stomach. He turned and kissed her.

"You want to go into the shack? Dex wouldn't mind."

"No." Mindy sighed, her voice becoming distant. "I've got to get home. My mom wants me there for dinner."

"I can bike you back."

"Naw. I kinda want to walk today."

They kissed one last time. Manson watched as she walked away. She disappeared into the forest like a phantom, walking through the trees. Manson sat alone for a while, letting the sun sink deeper in the sky. Eventually, he forced himself to get up.

He walked up to Dex, who was still sitting shirtless.

"You just got blue-balled, didn't ya?"

"What are you even doin' right now?" Manson asked passively.

"Working on my tan. I'm going to the beach with some friends tomorrow. I want to look good for all the guys."

"You have friends?"

"Really, dude?" Dex looked up at Manson, his face twisted in an odd expression. "That joke was so lame. I expect better from you." He sat up and stretched his arms. "How are you and Mindy doing?"

"Good."

"I'm still angry you introduced me to her at work."

"You'll get over it."

"Nope. The damage is permanent. I'll have to bring these emotional scars with me when I head down to Colorado."

Manson didn't like being reminded of the inevitable. Yet the inevitable always came, one way or another. He looked up at the quickly darkening sky. The pink edge at the top of the trees was rapidly sinking into the greenery.

Manson said goodbye to Dex and biked away. Dread filled him as he reached his house, slowly pedaling up the driveway. An unfamiliar car sat there. He could see the inside of the bright house through the drawn curtains. He heard his mother laughing. She was talking emphatically to someone who was hidden behind the edge of the window. Her smile was so wide and so happy. He couldn't remember the last time he'd seen her like that. Maybe he never had.

Manson wanted to sink into the dark. He wanted to be enveloped by the night and taken away with it. He wanted to stay an outsider to his mom's smile and the brightly lit house that surrounded her. But he couldn't. His feet pressed against the wooden steps, and his hand reached for the cold metal doorknob. The light from the house engulfed him as he let the door shut behind him.

The town hadn't changed much. Not that Dan had expected it to. It did look older. Like an old classmate who hadn't aged well. His tires dipped in and out of potholes with a dull thud. The buildings that once seemed so vibrant were now dull and lifeless. He wasn't sure whether the town had aged with him or he had aged past it.

He passed the high school and rolled over the train tracks. He recalled walking down them with Manson when they were younger. *How is Manson?* he wondered. He'd been thinking about his brother a lot. Dan puffed on a cigar as he contemplated. The smoke wafted out the car and into oblivion. He threw the rest of the cigar out the window as he entered the trailer park. Kids on bikes passed by, yelling obscenities at each other in a desperate attempt to seem older than they were.

Dan pulled into the driveway, his eyes surveying the run-down house. It was strange being back. He had been so eager to leave that he hadn't realized how much he missed the normalcy of home.

When he walked in, his mother greeted him with a warm hug. "It's so nice to see you!" she said, looking young and vibrant. She wore a flowery sundress, and her hair was tied in a braid. This wasn't the woman Dan remembered. She stepped back, looking him up and down. "My goodness! You're so much bigger!"

It was true. When Dan left home, he'd been scrawny. Now, his muscular form could barely be contained by his plain brown T-shirt and faded jeans. His smile was the only thing that had stayed the same. It was as joyful and boyish as ever.

His mom ushered him into a chair. "So how have things been?"

"It's been good." Dan's eyes wandered around the house. It was familiar yet alien. "The military's hard work, but I love it. Makes me feel like I'm doing something good in the world."

The conversation wore on for some time. His mother barraged him with question after question. It seemed like she was avoiding the most pressing question.

"How's Manson been handling Grandma's passing?" Dan asked abruptly. The elephant in the room had finally been addressed. His mother shifted uncomfortably in her chair. Dan suddenly felt like a stranger.

"He seems to be handling it well. We've both been grieving in our own ways."

"Where is he?"

She shifted uncomfortably again, her eyes downcast. "I think he's with friends. He does his own thing nowadays."

"I feel bad for not calling often enough." Dan watched his mother's movements. She seemed oddly formal. "I don't mean to be distant, but you know how it is when you get caught up in the day-to—" Dan was caught off guard as the door swung open. *"Manson?"*

His brother was taller than he remembered. His hair was long and shaggy, and he smelled strongly of cigarettes. If Dan had bulked up with time, Manson had thinned down. He looked almost skeletal. His face was long, but he had the same boyish handsomeness as his brother.

"Hey." His voice was deeper too.

Dan stood up, embracing his brother. Manson returned the hugged. Dan sensed a distance between them that a hug couldn't close. He couldn't shake the feeling that he was a stranger in his own home. "How have things been, man?"

"Fine." Manson stepped back, his long arms dangling awkwardly by his side.

"What have you been up to?"

"Working."

Dan couldn't help but feel annoyed at the one-word answers. "You wanna sit down and talk?"

"Naw." Manson rubbed the back of his head. "I gotta get up for work tomorrow. I better get some sleep."

"Manson, sit down and talk to your brother!" Dan was taken aback by his mother's vicious tone. "You haven't seen him in three years!"

"And that's somehow my fault?"

Dan did not like how quickly the situation was escalating.

"Sit down and talk to your brother!"

"Listen," Dan interjected, "it's not a big deal. Manson needs sleep."

"It *is* a big deal!" Their mother was yelling now, her eyes tearing up. She had wanted this to go perfectly. "Manson, do as I say!"

Manson laughed derisively. "Like you have any control over me. I'm the only one who makes any fucking money around here." The anger in Manson's eyes cut through Dan in a profound way. This was not the brother he remembered. "You're the one who should be doing as she's told!"

"Hey!" Dan's voice was louder than either of theirs. "That's our mother!"

Manson laughed again. His snide chuckle burrowed under Dan's skin. "Who the fuck are you to tell me shit? You get back after three years, and you think you're the man of the house all of a sudden?"

"Manson," Dan said, his eyes sincere and earnest, "what the hell is wrong with you?"

Manson stood, silenced. The question was asked so honestly, it didn't seem like an insult. Dan looked at his brother in utter confusion and dismay. *What kind of man has this boy turned into?*

"Fuck this shit." Manson walked out of the house, letting the dark consume him.

Dan turned to his mother, puzzled. This was not the same home he had left.

Manson rode away, his heart pounding and his mind racing. He was trying to figure out what had just happened. It was all a blur. He'd spat out words that were not his own. They'd come from a place ruled by instinct, a place he was incapable of fully comprehending.

Manson rode fast, the adrenaline from the confrontation still pounding in his head. The warm night air blew dark shadows about. Moonlight was the only thing that guided him down dark country streets. He was going to the only place he understood anymore, the place that came closest to what he considered a home.

He tripped his way through the dark forest. His feet kept getting caught on shrubbery that reached out like fingers in the dark. The branches overhead leaned down at him like a gothic cloud. He threw his bike down outside the shack and stumbled in, leaving the door open. He fell down on the couch, his heart pounding in his chest.

He reached for his phone and scrolled through his contacts. Once he found her name, he pressed dial. The phone rang for what seemed like a lifetime. Finally, he heard her voice.

"Hello?"

"Mindy." Manson's voice cracked.

Mindy saw the glare of her alarm clock from under her sheets. She was tucked beneath them like an unborn child, hiding in her mother's womb. It was past two in the morning, yet she still lay awake. The knife blade in her hand kept her from sleep.

She brushed it gently against her skin. She didn't press hard enough to cut flesh, only hard enough to feel like she could. She had promised not to cut herself. But she liked to know she could, if she really wanted to. She liked to feel the blade against her skin. It soothed her. It was always in the dead of the night that she played with the blade. That way, only the shadows could judge her.

The phone by Mindy's bedside suddenly jumped to life with a startling intensity. She jumped in surprise, her hand jerking the knife blade into her skin. She cradled the wound as the phone continued ringing. She prayed and hoped that the cut didn't leave a mark. Her mom would think she was cutting again.

Mindy threw the covers off and pressed a piece of tissue against the wound. She answered the phone, holding it against her ear with her shoulder. Who would be calling at this time?

"Mindy?" The voice was weak and vulnerable.

"Manson?"

"I need you." His voice vibrated with emotion. Mindy could almost see his body shaking. Without another word spoken, she understood what he meant. Something had happened. The night was old, but the morning was new, and she wanted to be by his side.

"Where are you?"

"The shack."

"I'm on my way."

She hung up and crept out her room. Silently, she exited the apartment and slinked down into the parking lot. The streetlights guided her through the ghostly town. At night, it almost seemed haunted. The country roads were even less appealing with their shadowy demeanor. The trees hid in the dark, like figures disappearing once light found them.

She drove as far into the forest as she could. She left the car running, the headlights guiding her down the narrow path. The light faded as she approached the shack. The door hung open, battering against the exterior.

"Manson?" She closed the door behind her.

"Mindy?"

She heard him but did not see him. "Do you have a light?"

He turned on his cell phone, the blue light casting an eerie glow across his face.

"What's the matter?" Mindy asked as she sat next to her boyfriend. She caressed his face with her soft palm. He leaned into it gently, like a tired puppy wanting to be petted.

"My brother ... it didn't go well."

The statement was simple, but Mindy understood. "What happened?"

"I don't know. I just ... I just exploded. I don't know why." Mindy moved closer. Her thighs brushed against him, sending a tingle up his spine. The thoughts and angst that had been plaguing his mind evaporated in an instant. He sighed in relief. His body relaxed in a way he couldn't explain. "You make everything better."

The statement lit up Mindy's insides. She kissed him passionately.

Manson's hands began finding their way around her curves, but something stopped him. A cold trickle was on her wrist. Manson gently pushed her away. His fingers caressed her blood-spattered wrist. "Why do you do this?" he asked tenderly.

"There ... there are a lot of reasons." She wiped the blood onto the old cushions. "Sometimes it's because I feel numb. Like there's nothing inside me. Most of the time, it's because I feel ... this distance. Like there's a wall between me and the people around me. Like I'm not part of this world." Mindy looked up at Manson with big eyes. "When I'm with you ... I don't feel that distance."

They continued kissing, more and more passionately. Mindy leaned backward until she was lying down with Manson on top of her. Manson's hands wandered around her body, his heart pounding with passion and his mind flooded with emotion.

INTERLUDE

I felt a man inside me. A man I love. His body merged with mine to make something whole. His hands wandered around every curve with the delicacy of lust tamed. I felt what it meant to be someone to someone.

And I also felt fright.

Fright when his hands brushed against the mass of scar tissue that enveloped my thigh. The bumpy mass that always reminds me of who I really am behind the mask of joy that life occasionally places over my features.

It scared me, him touching who I really am. I gasped, wondering what he would say. Wondering what I should say. Then he leaned over, his warm breath caressing my ear.

"It's okay."

A whisper so quiet it was like the voice that rests in your head. And as he whispered, his body plunged into mine. I gasped again, my fingers finding his lips and sliding into them.

"It's okay."

It'll always be okay.

—Mindy
(Journal Excerpt)

What makes us stay
Inside pain?
Why don't we
Push it away?
What makes us stay
Inside sorrow?
What makes us
This way?

—Mindy

SEVEN

The trailer park's streets were cracked and gnarled. Manson pedaled through them, the wheels of his bike treading softly. He looked up. The pink sky was darkening. Home was just a few blocks away. He didn't want to be there. Mom and Grandma had been arguing a lot lately.

Night fell, and Manson could no longer procrastinate. Reluctantly, he headed home.

He could hear the two of them arguing from the driveway. He sat motionless on his bike, staring at the window. The curtains were drawn, but the light from the other side shone through. He liked standing outside. It made him feel like the life inside wasn't his.

"What are you doing?"

Manson hadn't noticed Dan standing on the porch. He was smoking. He must have stolen cigarettes from Mom again.

Manson sighed. "You know …"

"Yeah, I do." Dan put out the cigarette and threw it aside. "Wanna go for a walk?"

"Sure."

They stopped by the gas station to get some snacks. After a while of wandering around town, they found themselves walking the train tracks. Even in the dark, they found their way to the cliff. The town hung below them, the streetlights gleaming like distant stars.

"Excited for freshman year?"

Manson shrugged. "School's just school."

"High school's different." Dan sat cross-legged, while Manson's feet hung over the cliff's edge.

"How?" Manson banged his heels against the rock face.

"The girls get hotter."

Manson chuckled. "That's it?"

"There's a lot that's different. You just have to experience it."

"If you say so." Manson looked over at his brother. The tip of his cigarette glowed in the night. "Can I try it?"

"You're a high schooler now." Dan blew smoke. He handed his brother the cig. They sat for a while longer, the night moving around them.

Dan didn't know what to do. He had comforted his mom after the confrontation with Manson. She seemed to shrink into herself. The next day she was sitting in front of the TV, smoking. The shades had been drawn, and her smile was gone. The glare of the screen made her look older than she was. Dan tried to lure her out of whatever state she was in, but she seemed content to stay where she was. They talked for a while, but no matter how hard he tried, they'd both end up just staring at the TV. He quickly grew restless.

"Where's Manson?" Dan asked.

"Probably at work."

"Does he still work at the gas station?"

"I think so." She let the butt of her cigarette fall into an ashtray and reached for another one.

Dan wandered around town. He couldn't sit in that dingy house any longer. He puffed on a cigar, letting the cracked sidewalks lead him. He found himself in the local bar, talking to old friends who still drank there. He stopped by the high school to see old teachers. He went to random stores. No matter what he did, he still felt restless. The civilian life wasn't for him.

As Dan walked up and down the length of the town, he glanced at the gas station now and again. He stood across from it as evening came, trying to build the courage to go inside. Was Manson even working? But where else could he be? Dan replayed the conversation from the night before over and over in his head, trying to think of something to say to make things right.

Before Dan could summon the courage, two figures emerged from the station. Manson walked hand in hand with a young black girl. He watched as they kissed, apparently said good night, and departed. It was then that Dan was overcome by the profound knowledge that he knew absolutely nothing about his brother's life.

Dan marched across the street. Manson didn't see him approach. He mounted his bike and threw a cigarette butt to the ground. When he looked up, his brother was standing in front of him. Manson felt a surge of something close to fear—a mixture of embarrassment and anger with a side of adrenaline.

Before he could say anything Dan spoke up.

"Where did you go last night? Mom and I were worried sick!"

Manson interpreted the question more aggressively than Dan meant it. Manson glared at his brother. "You shouldn't worry. I'm a grown man. I can handle myself." Manson pushed off on his bike, ready to leave his brother in the dust.

"Wait!" Dan reached out, stopping his brother. Manson felt a surge of anger as Dan grabbed his shoulder. "Listen … what happened last night … whatever that was … let's forget about it. It didn't happen. Let's act like this is the first time we've seen each other."

A silence followed that words couldn't breach. The brothers stared at each other, trying to find something to say.

Words formed deep within Dan's gut, but they got caught in his throat on the way up. "There's nothing you want to say?" Those were the only words Dan could get out of his clogged throat.

"There's a lot I want to say." The statement was bitter and cutting.

"Then just say it. Clear the air."

Manson chuckled snidely, a smart-ass grin on his face. "What the hell did you expect to happen when you came back?" The words slithered from Manson's mouth like snakes. "Did you think everything would be the same as when you left?"

"Of course I didn't!" Dan exclaimed. "But I sure as hell wasn't expecting this!"

"And what is *this* to you?" Manson spat out the words.

Dan sighed, resigning himself to the fact that he couldn't avoid confrontation with his brother. "Why are you still here?" Dan motioned around him. "This town is a shit-hole. You were an A student in school. You could have gone anywhere, done anything."

The bitterness that had been resting in Manson's soul suddenly bubbled to the surface. It surrounded his heart like a clenched fist and flowed through his veins and into his mind like the sizzling ash of a volcano. "You really are fucking blind, aren't you?"

Dan looked his brother up and down. "You've changed."

In a sudden burst of anger, Manson jumped off his bike and threw it to the ground. Dan took a step back in surprise. Anger permeated every orifice of Manson's being. His eyes bulged to the point that they seemed prepared to jump from their sockets. "Why am I still here? Why the *fuck* am I still here?" Manson pounded his index finger against his chest as he shouted. Dan looked around, afraid someone might see his hysterical sibling. "You were in such a hurry to leave, you didn't notice what was going on around you!"

"Listen … just calm down. Let's go home, and we can discuss this."

"You left right when Mom lost her job!" Manson pressed on, ignoring his brother. "If you haven't fucking noticed, she never found a new one! And guess who had to start paying the bills? It sure as hell wasn't you!"

"Why didn't you tell me!" Dan asked defensively. "I could have sent money!"

"Yeah, because we've talked *so* much over the last three years, haven't we?"

"Listen …" Dan said tentatively, "I'm sorry. If you let me explain—"

"No, you listen!" Manson's face was red with rage. "And don't pretend like you're sorry! You're happy you left! You're happy you made it out of this shit town! If you had the chance to do it over, you'd do the same damn thing! You'd leave me to take care of a dying grandmother and an unemployed hack of a mom!"

Dan stood silent for a moment, letting Manson's words hang in the air while he formulated a response. "You're right … I wouldn't change a thing."

The words hit Manson hard. The rage inside him grew, but with it came a mix of emotions—betrayal, confusion, and a tinge of sadness. His hands were shaking with the adrenaline that pulsated through his veins. "You're a fucking coward." Manson threw the words at his brother with resentment.

"Maybe I am," Dan admitted. "Maybe I'm just an asshole who runs away from his problems. But if I'm a coward, so are you. You're a coward for staying here."

"How fucking dare you." The words were a sinister whisper. "I stayed here because I had to! You think Mom was going to take care of Grandma? She can barely take care of herself."

"They are not your responsibility!" Dan was now yelling in earnest. "They're not mine either. I got the hell out of this town because I needed to live my life! You need to do the same."

"How the hell do you sleep at night? Our grandma just died, and you talk about this family like it's a burden to you."

"Don't pretend, Manson. Mom never supported us. Grandma did her best, but she could only do so much. We fended for ourselves our whole childhood. Have you forgotten that?"

"If you hated this family so much, why did you even bother to come back?"

Flabbergasted and exhausted with the conversation, Dan rubbed his tired hands against his temples and sighed. "I never said I hated this family. You'll always *be* my family. But this town ... this place ... living at home ... it's unhealthy. You need to move on."

"How could I, when Grandma was sick? She was dying."

"Manson!" Dan yelled, this time in anger. "That's just an excuse you made for yourself. Grandma was sick, but you being here wasn't going to change that. It *didn't* change that."

Manson's heartbeat increased as Dan spoke. It was like a pounding drum. Every beat filled Manson with more and more rage. He felt himself losing control. Dan's words infected his ears like worms, wriggling into his brain and festering. Manson lurched forward suddenly without a sound and pressed his shoulder violently into Dan's stomach, knocking the wind out of him. There was a loud thump as they both fell backward and hit the concrete pavement. Dan was stunned for a moment, caught completely off guard.

Manson sat up on his knees, his legs on either side of his brother's torso. He raised his fist high and sent it flying toward Dan's face. His plan immediately backfired. Pain surged up his arm as his knuckles hit concrete. Dan had moved his head quickly to avoid the impact. Tears welled in Manson's eyes as his knuckles pulsated with pain.

Dan easily threw his brother off and stood up. Manson stumbled to his feet, waiting for his brother's attack.

Instead, Dan looked at him, appalled. "What the fuck is wrong with you?"

Manson looked for something to say but was at a loss. He jumped on his bike and rode away, with his brother's eyes burning into his back.

"I love you."
The things these words can do.
"I love you too."
These words consume
All that you
Are.

—Mindy

EIGHT

Mindy stood outside the school, her fragile eyes looking down at the pavement and her fingers locked into the straps of her backpack. She heard girls behind her, their shallow chatter drawing no interest from her. Her feet scraped the pavement; the bottoms of her shoes were worn with age.

"Oh look, it's the wrist-bleeder."

Mindy looked up as three girls approached. Leading the way was a blonde, who, despite her young age, had makeup caked on her face.

Mindy sighed. "Susan, do you ever stop to think about how much you sound like a B-list Disney villain?"

"Oh, the wrist-bleeder talks."

Mindy laughed. "You want something?"

"I want you to admit you're a fucking freak."

Mindy shrugged. "Okay. I'm a freak."

Susan paused, unsure how to respond. "That's not something you should be proud of."

"You shouldn't be proud that you managed to raid your mom's makeup cabinet and lather it on your face like some kind of hungover Barbie doll."

"What does *lather* mean?" one of the girls asked.

Mindy looked at her. "Not surprising, coming from the girl who failed English twice."

"Show us your wrists, freak."

Mindy happily put her wrists forward. Susan looked for a clever retort, but her immaturity clogged her throat. She walked away, with her friends convincing her she'd won some kind of arbitrary victory.

Mindy skipped out of the forest, her wide smile still fresh from a lingering kiss. The evening sky illuminated the shack in a translucent way. It looked almost like a picture you'd find hanging in the back of a thrift shop. Dex was outside, wearing nothing but a ragged pair of blue jeans. He was crouched down, with a bottle of red spray paint in his hands. His finger held down the button as his hands moved fluidly.

"I didn't know you painted." Mindy's voice was perky and alive, like a bright sunflower.

"I don't." Dex sounded surprisingly serious, not his jovial self.

Mindy leaned over to see what he was painting. She stifled a chuckle as she looked over a series of badly drawn penises. They looked like something an edgy elementary-school student would draw on the inside of his binder.

"Don't laugh," Dex commanded. "This is deadly serious."

"Is this what you're like when you're not high?" Mindy lightly jabbed.

"How do you know I'm not?" An edge of friendliness crept back into Dex's voice, but he remained focused on his work.

"I can just tell."

"Where's Manson?"

"He's riding his bike. He'll be here soon."

As if summoning him from the forest, Manson emerged. Mindy's heart suddenly dropped. She could tell, even from a distance, that something was wrong. Her fears were confirmed when she saw his tear-stained cheeks.

She jogged up to him, wiping her thumb gently under his eyes. "What's the matter, honey?"

"My brother ... he was there after you left."

"What did he say? What happened?"

Manson sighed. "We can talk about it later. I'm not in the mood right now."

Mindy pushed her concern away and kissed Manson. He took her hand and walked over to Dex. Manson felt a little better with his fingers wrapped around Mindy's knuckles.

Manson looked down at Dex's paintings in familiar disbelief. "What the fuck are you doing?"

"I'm preparing."

"What the hell for?"

Dex stood up, spinning the spray can in his hand. "Revenge."

Manson rolled his eyes. He had been friends with Dex long enough to know when he had criminal intent. "Okay, tell me what the hell is going on."

"You know when I said I was going to the beach with my friends? Turns out they weren't really my friends." Dex turned toward Mindy and pointed, using the can as an index finger. "You want to be the driver?"

"Driver? Where are we driving?"

"You know where Northlane is?"

"The gated community outside of town?"

"That's the one!" Dex smiled his signature silly grin. "We ride at nightfall."

"Hold your fucking horses." Manson brought the conversation back down to earth. "We ain't doing shit until you tell us what's going on."

Dex's smile disappeared as he rubbed his scalp therapeutically. "Listen … bottom line is I got a prank pulled on me. Now it's my turn."

Mindy nudged Dex gently. "You can tell us what happened."

He reluctantly gave in. "Well … understand that when this happened, I was shit-faced drunk. Basically … I got fooled into entering a porta-potty, and … well …."

Manson held his breath in anticipation, knowing this next part was going to be good.

"They rolled it down a dune into Lake Michigan."

Manson burst out laughing. Dex's face became beet red, a mixture of anger and embarrassment.

Mindy pulled at her boyfriend's hand gently. "Hey … come on," she said softly. "That's not funny."

"How the hell did they trick you?" Manson wheezed out between fits of laughter. Dex's face went even redder. "Oh, this has to be good." Manson smiled widely. "What did they tempt you with? A blow job or something?"

The shade of red on Dex's face became so deep it almost seemed unnatural. "He was really attractive."

"You weren't even drunk, were you?" Manson couldn't stop his laughter. "Blow job in a porta-potty! That's some classy shit, man!"

Mindy walked over to Dex and hugged him. "I'm sorry," she said genuinely.

"You don't have to be." Dex's tone was serious again. "Because you guys are going to help me get them back."

"What are we talking about here?" Manson asked, finally controlling his guffawing. "What kind of revenge?"

Dex smiled. "I have it all planned out."

Mindy's headlights led them down barren country roads. She weaved through the countryside, with rows of corn on either side. Dex gave Mindy directions as she drove, eventually leading her down a creepy dirt path. The light from the car only made the surrounding dark more unsettling. They parked on the side of the road. With a shudder, the car was silenced as Mindy pulled the keys out.

"Put these on." Dex handed Manson and Mindy black hoods, which they pulled over their faces.

"Great. Now I feel like a criminal," Mindy joked as they stepped out of the car.

"If you're not feeling up to it, you can stay in the car," Dex said, missing her humor. "Things are about to get real. We don't need someone getting in our way."

Mindy bristled. "I'm fine."

Dex rummaged around in the trunk. He pulled out several rolls of toilet paper and shoved them into a bag. He then grabbed a large brick with a note tied to it.

"I can't believe we're doing this." Mindy didn't realize she had said the words out loud until it was too late.

Dex pounced on her. "Are you sure you don't want to stay in the car?"

"Yes. Stop treating me like a child."

They walked down the dirt road for a while, and then Dex led them into the dark forest. The dim flashlight he held was the only thing to guide them. Manson held the bag of toilet paper in one hand and Mindy's sweaty palm in the other. She prayed that her rapidly beating heart wasn't pulsating down her arm and into Manson's.

"Why are you shaking so much?" he asked.

"I'm cold." It was an obvious lie, considering the sweat streaming down her forehead.

Manson led her a little way away from Dex and spoke to her privately in a hushed tone. "If you're uncomfortable with this, we can bail. Dex and I can do this later. You don't have to be involved."

"No, I want to be involved." She said it more to reassure herself than Manson. "It's just that … I've never done anything like this before. I'm a straight-A student. The most rebellious thing I've ever done is turn in a homework assignment late."

"I was a straight-A student, and I still did stuff like this." Manson was doing his best to reassure her. "Then again, without Dex's being my friend, I probably would have been just like you."

"What am I *just like?*" Mindy waited for the answer longer than she would have liked.

Manson looked up at the dark branches that swayed overhead. He contemplated the answer as the moon cast its judgment down on him. "You're beautiful."

"Is that all I am?" Mindy was happy with the compliment, but she decided to give Manson hell anyway. "Just a pretty face?"

"Beauty is more than that." Their steps crunched lightly against fallen twigs. "It's everything about you—the way you carry yourself, your personality … everything."

It was as if a warm candle had been lit at the center of Mindy's soul. She leaned her head against Manson's arm and said, as gentle as the breeze, "I love you."

"I love you too."

The candle burst into a warm flame. The fear she had felt only moments ago was replaced. But, as always, a small voice in her head told her this wasn't real. She ignored it for now.

Dex abruptly switched the flashlight off. "We're getting closer." They could see lights in the distance, and they stumbled toward them together. The nighttime darkness suddenly seemed more ominous. They eventually reached a tall brick wall. They could see the light of streetlamps on the other side.

"Gated community?" Manson questioned. "It looks more like a damn fortress."

"I'll go up first," Dex said in a hushed tone. "I'll give you the all-clear."

Dex climbed up a nearby tree with surprising agility. He jumped from one shadowy branch to the next until he could perch himself on the wall. "Come on up," he whispered loudly.

Manson turned toward Mindy. "This is your last chance to turn back."

She smiled. "Never."

Pointless people with pointless lives,
Empty vessels trying to describe
Why they are important to a world that does not care.
Screaming that it isn't fair
Before they sink into oblivion and disappear
Forever.

—Mindy

NINE

The fourth-grade classroom was full of chatter. Manson sat in the back, staring at his desk. His leg twitched nervously. The first day of school was always the worst, especially when Manson was stuck in a class without either of his friends.

"Hey."

Manson looked up. A strange kid with long black hair slid into the chair next to him. He smelled weird.

"Hey," Manson said quietly.

"All these kids are stupid."

Manson laughed. "Yeah."

"I'm Dex." The boy nodded, his long hair bouncing.

"Manson."

"Like the serial killer?"

"Uh … no."

"I like serial killers. My dad watches documentaries about them."

"Oh."

"I hate school," Dex exclaimed, pulling out a shabby-looking notebook. Manson couldn't help but notice the crude drawings scribbled on the front. "I sat next to you 'cause I can tell you're smart."

"Thanks." Manson's voice came out as a whisper.

"I'm going to copy off you for the rest of the school year."

"Oh ... okay."

Dex smiled. "We're going to be friends."

The streetlamps illuminated well-paved streets and unnaturally pristine lawns. Fancy cars sat in driveways with nice houses towering above them. Three suspicious figures walked the street, avoiding the lamplight. They stayed hunkered down next to the hedge line as they crawled silently through the neighborhood that looked plucked from a magazine cover.

Dex led the way, followed by Manson, who held a tight grip on Mindy's hand. Her heart pounded in excitement as her eyes drifted around the neighborhood. She was officially an accomplice, a role she was not accustomed to.

In the middle of the town was a particularly nice house that stood out from the rest. Its hedges were tall, blocking most of the house from view. The only way to see the house was through the large gate in front of the driveway. Its lawn was extravagant with full-grown trees. The house itself was four stories high with a multitude of windows, all of which were dark.

"We're here," Dex whispered.

Manson peered through the gates. "How did you make friends with rich kids?"

"The thing about rich kids is they're too chicken to buy their own weed."

"How do we get in?" Mindy asked.

"There should be a weak spot in the hedge." Dex shoved his hands into the greenery as Manson and Mindy looked around, making sure they weren't spotted. "Through here." They pushed through the hedge, the small twig-like branches cutting softly against their skin.

"Who the hell needs a lawn this big?" Manson whispered.

"Rich pricks." Dex set the bag of toilet paper on the lawn. "You guys cover as much ground as you can. You've got your job; I've got mine. When you see me running toward the front, you book it. Got it?"

Mindy and Manson nodded.

"All right, get going." Dex took off, disappearing into shadow.

Manson picked up a roll of toilet paper and threw it up over a tree. The moonlight shimmered against its surface. It fell to the ground gently, one long strip of white covering the green leaves. Manson smiled at Mindy. "Come on!" His voice was a raspy whisper that held a boyish excitement. Mindy joined in, and soon the whole tree was covered. They moved on to the next and the next and then started covering the ground. Mindy kept glancing at the house, making sure that the lights didn't suddenly flicker to life.

"You still nervous?" Manson asked quietly.

"Not really." Mindy threw a roll down the length of the lawn.

"Your hands are still shaking," Manson observed.

"It's not that I'm scared; it's just that …" Mindy looked at the house. "We could get caught at any second. The lights could flash on, and we'd be done for. I would get a record, maybe go to jail, maybe miss out on college …"

"So you are scared."

"No … but our lives could change forever. For better or worse, they'd change. One decision, one second—boom. Your life is flipped upside down."

"In my experience"—Manson crumpled toilet paper into a ball—"life moves much slower." He threw it playfully at Mindy. It unrolled and tangled in her hair. She feigned annoyance and threw a whole roll at him. He dodged it easily.

"You've never had a life-changing moment?" Mindy asked.

"Sure I have. Everyone has. But after every big moment, there are ten thousand small ones that follow. The small moments drown out the big ones. In fact, the big moments are only there to make you realize how boring the rest of life is."

"Well, you're just full of positivity, aren't you," Mindy quipped.

"The only difference in how I view the world and how someone else views it is that I'm honest about it."

Mindy's eyes darted away from Manson. She rubbed her wrists self-consciously.

Manson noticed the motion. His eyes were drawn to the scars. He decided to ask the question he'd been wondering for some time. "Do you still cut?"

Mindy looked across the lawn. Not much grass was showing through the layers of white. She felt herself unravelling as she dropped the last roll of toilet paper and let it bounce away. "Sometimes," she admitted.

"Why?"

Mindy inhaled deeply, taking in the moist night air and exhaling slowly. "I don't know. I ... I just think my brain works differently. I've suffered from depression my whole life. They try to give me meds for it, but I ... I just can't."

"Why can't you?"

"I've tried taking them; I really have." Her eyes were fixed in a distant gaze. "Meds make me feel ... different. I don't like it. Maybe ... maybe I've become so accustomed to the sadness that I can't live any other way. Maybe I'm supposed to be like this. Broken."

Manson looked at Mindy. Her eyes had misted over as she'd opened up to him. She looked like a ghost, standing there in the dark. "What makes you sad?" Manson asked; he truly wanted to know.

"I don't know. It's just ..." Mindy thought long and hard before answering. "People go about their day-to-day lives as if their actions matter. As if they're making some kind of monumental impact. As if ... they have some ultimate purpose. But how can they when this—everything—leads to their bodies being six feet under? How can you think that what you do matters when there are countless people all over this planet, just like you, rushing about, thinking they're important? Doesn't it just seem like ... it's all pointless?"

Manson was struck by her words. "Yes."

Mindy's head snapped toward him, her trance suddenly broken.

"I feel that way all the time," he said.

"I truly do love you," she said in a hushed tone as she embraced Manson in a kiss. They stood lip-locked with the profound knowledge that they understood what most did not.

The sound of breaking glass brought the couple crashing back into the present. Dex came sprinting around the corner, mouthing the word *run.* Manson grabbed Mindy's hand and took off. The darkened windows flashed to life, and they heard voices hiding behind the walls.

The trio struggled through the thick hedge, emerging on the other side with twigs entangled in their hair. They sprinted down the street, unconcerned with being stealthy. The neighborhood rustled from its slumber. Lights flickered on as they ran. They didn't dare look back.

They reached the wall quickly. Breathing heavily, they stopped in their tracks. "There!" Dex exclaimed. There was a tree in a neighboring lawn that reached up over the wall. They darted toward it, with Manson ushering Mindy up first.

As she climbed, her heart pounding with adrenaline, she looked out over the neighborhood. She could see the yard covered in toilet paper. Small figures stood yelling in outrage, one of them holding a brick in his hands. Mindy could also see a large penis was spray-painted on the side of the house.

Manson crawled up next, perching next to Mindy on the wall. They watched Dex crawl through the branches, their nervous eyes looking over the neighborhood that was now bustling with life. A long stream of light was suddenly cast over the lawn. A fat man stumbled out his front door, holding a shotgun. Mindy and Manson gasped in horror.

"Dex!" they screamed.

He looked over just in time to see the barrel pointed his way. The shot echoed through the night. Dex fell backward, and tree bark flew through the air. He fell onto the lawn, his ears ringing but largely unharmed. The man ran over, pointing the gun down at Dex.

"Don't move!" he threatened, his voice heavy with breath as his chins waggled.

Dex looked up, relieved to see his friends had already fled into the forest.

Bloodlines mingle.
Family and friends are the same.
The one stain that remains
On the world you will eventually leave.
They are the reason you breathe,
They are the one thing you need.
But even they fade when you fade,
And you're left to debate,
Whether or not it was worth it.
Was it worth it?

—Mindy

TEN

Manson stood staring at his bike. The wheel was bent badly, and the chain had come loose and lay haphazardly on the concrete. His eye was black and his body bruised. His fists were clenched, as were his teeth. The train tracks sat nearby, their gleaming metal stained with some of his blood.

A car came around the bend in the road and slowly pulled up. Dan lowered the passenger-side window, his eyes peering at his brother from behind sunglasses. Manson continued staring at his broken bike.

"Who did this?"

Blood dripped from Manson's nose and mixed with the slobber on his lips. "Some of your buddies from the football team."

"Which way did they go?"

Manson pointed down the street.

"Throw the bike in the back."

Dan's knuckles were wrapped tightly around the steering wheel as he drove. They were a deep white by the time they came upon the football players. Manson could see his bloody reflection in the windshield as they drew closer to the players.

"What are you going to do?" Manson asked.

Dan was silent.

Dan pulled up to a dramatic stop and parked in front of the kids. They looked a bit surprised as Dan hopped out, sunglasses hiding his steely complexion. The leader of the pack chuckled, his shoulders rising with the motion.

"Dan the man." His voice was high-pitched and didn't match his masculine physique. "What's hanging—"

Dan cocked his hand back and swung as hard as he could. Blood gushed from the boy's mouth as he fell to the ground. The other two kids stood back, wide eyed and astonished. Dan stomped on the kid until he was sure there was no fight left in him. Reaching down, he grabbed the boy's wallet, taking out a wad of cash. "For the bike repairs." He threw the wallet on the ground as the kid rolled over, groaning. Dan looked at the other two.

"Hey, man," one of them said, taking a few steps back and holding his hands up in surrender. "We didn't know you knew the kid."

"He's my brother." There were a few seconds of silence. "I'll see you all at practice." Dan walked back to the car.

A few hours later, Dan sat in the driveway with Manson. The bent tire sat on the lawn as they screwed on the new one.

"Thanks for this," Manson said quietly.

Dan did not respond. His eyes were still hidden behind black lenses.

"Are you ... are you angry at me?"

"No," Dan said as he spun the wheel, making sure it worked. "I'm just worried."

"About what?"

Dan sighed, taking off his sunglasses. "What are you going to do when I can't help you?"

Manson found it hard to look his brother in the eye.

"Look at me."

Manson forced his gaze to meet his brother's.

"I know they're bigger than you. I know they're stronger. But do whatever you have to do to survive. To win. Bite, scratch, kick them in the balls. You need to learn how to fight back. How to stand up for yourself. I won't always be there to save your ass."

"I know," Manson said weakly.

"Hey," Dan reassured, "I'm not angry. Really. I just hate to see this happen to you."

"Thanks."

"Okay." Dan sighed, slipping his sunglasses back on. "Let's take this fucker for a test-drive."

They ran through the forest, their breath heavy and their lungs burning. Their hearts pounded in unison as adrenaline flooded their veins. Twigs and dead leaves flew through the air as their feet slammed into the ground, only to take flight the next second. Somehow, the night didn't hinder them. They flew through it like moving shadows. Manson skidded to a stop as he hit the road, his feet leaving streaks in the sand. Mindy burst from the foliage after him. She leaned over in exhaustion, her breath as heavy as her heart.

"Dex ..." she spat out between breaths. "Dex ... will he ... be okay?"

Manson exhaled. "I don't know."

"What do we do?"

Manson ripped off his hood and ran his hands through his sweaty hair. "We can't do anything."

Mindy lifted her hood, revealing a sweaty face that gleamed in the moonlight. "We need to do something!"

"What?" Manson exclaimed in frustration. "What should we do? Go back? Get caught along with him?"

"What if that man shoots him?" Mindy was nearly in tears. "What if he dies?"

Manson embraced Mindy's shoulders warmly. Her concerned face gleamed at him through the darkness of night. He kissed her forehead lightly. Salty sweat rested on his lips.

"He'll be fine. That man will call the police, and Dex will be arrested."

"What then?"

"Dex has a record. He could go to jail for a while, or he could be placed on probation. He'll be fine. He's been through worse."

Mindy closed her eyes, her face still contorted in concern. Her head fell against Manson's chest. She hoped that when she opened her eyes she'd wake from the terrible nightmare she had fallen into.

"Come on ... let's go," Manson said.

They walked down the road, the black sky bleeding into blue.

They spent the night in the shack. Their sleep was restless.

Later the next morning, Manson explained, "Dex and I are partners in crime. We've done things—not-so-legal things—together before. And we've been caught more than once. They'll come looking for me if they suspect Dex wasn't alone. I've got to lie low. I'll stay here for a while."

"You can't stay here like this." Mindy lightly lifted Manson's grubby shirt, which was soaked with cold sweat. "You're dirty, and you smell like shit." She smiled, and her words somehow became a compliment. "Come home with me. My parents will be at work. We can shower."

Manson smiled and kissed her. "You in the shower—I like the sound of that."

Their dirty clothes tumbled in the wash as their hands felt each other under the rush of warm water. Misty steam surrounded them in the small bathroom, blocking their view of each other. They didn't see; they just felt. Afterward, they lay on Mindy's bed, their clothes still warm from the dryer. They watched television, happy just to be in each other's company.

"I'm still thinking about Dex," Mindy admitted.

"Me too."

Mindy's head rested on Manson's arm. The bright-pink room and fluffy white sheets surrounded them like a picture from a storybook. The space smelled of roses and perfume.

"Your room is nicer than my entire house."

Mindy smiled. "It's because I have style and you don't."

"The sass is unbearable," Manson quipped as he kissed her. The kiss began developing into more, but Mindy pulled back as they heard the apartment door open.

"Looks like you're about to meet my family."

The bedroom door was suddenly flung open. "A boy!" Mindy's little brother, no older than six or seven, burst into the room. His head had been shaved, but a thin layer of hair had grown back. His grin was wide, revealing missing teeth. "Mindy's got a boy in her room!"

Mindy threw a pillow at him. "Get out of here, you brat!"

He giggled happily and ran down the hall, screaming, "Mindy's got a boy in her room! Mindy's got a boy in her room!"

A large woman suddenly popped her head around the corner, her chubby cheeks forming a wide smile. The resemblance to the boy was uncanny. "Why, hello!" She had a slight lisp and funny-looking eyes that wandered away from each other. When she walked in, her large form scraped against the door frame.

"I'm Manson." He jumped up awkwardly, although the cushy bed tried to suck him back. He shook hands with the woman.

"I like him already," the woman exclaimed. "So polite!"

"Mom ... you're embarrassing," Mindy said in a flat tone.

"No, I'm not! I'm not embarrassing, am I, Manson?"

"No, not at all." Even as Manson reassured the woman, his face went red.

"What's this I hear about a boy?" A muscular man came charging into the room, his head nearly scraping the ceiling. "Do I need to grab the shotgun?"

Mindy buried her face in a pillow, trying to hide from the embarrassment.

"Richard!" Mindy's mother said, slapping him lightly on the stomach. "Stop being silly! This is Manson, a fine young man."

"Nice to meet you," Manson said, extending his hand. Richard grabbed it in a tight lock and pumped it up and down. Manson felt as if his fingers were about to pop off.

"I like a boy with respect."

Manson pulled his hand back, moving his fingers to make sure they still worked.

"I'm Felicia, and this is Richard." The woman motioned toward her husband. "Would you care to join our family for dinner?"

"Of course!" Manson really wasn't sure if he had an option.

"Mindy, get your head out of that pillow," Richard shouted, louder than he'd intended. "Your boy is politer than you are."

Mindy meekly raised her head, her face beet red. "Promise you won't be this embarrassing at dinner."

No such promise was made. Dinner was full of loud exclamations over mashed potatoes and slabs of chicken. Manson tried laying low, navigating the chaos with caution.

"So how did you two meet?" Felicia asked as Manson politely scooped a spoonful of mashed potatoes.

"We both work at the gas station," Mindy answered.

"I knew that job would be good for you," Richard exclaimed proudly. "When you work, God provides!"

"He provided you with a man this time." Felicia looked at Manson, who smiled awkwardly.

Mindy face-palmed. "You guys are so embarrassing."

Her parents continued to drop embarrassing comments into the conversation, but as Manson adapted to the family's rhythm, he began to find it charming. The loud exclamations and cheerful talk were foreign to him, but he slipped comfortably into the conversation. As the warmness of the room seeped into him, he felt Mindy's warm touch from under the table. Her hand enveloped his as he gently nudged her leg. They smiled and continued without trepidation in the conversation.

After dinner, they went back to Mindy's room and relaxed under the cool glow of the TV.

"I think they like you," Mindy said, her voice heavy from a full day.

"I hope so." Manson shifted against the soft cushion. "I like them."

"They can"—Mindy paused thoughtfully—"be a lot to take in."

"You're lucky."

"How so?"

They both stared at the TV screen.

"I never had what you have—the conversations around a dinner table. The closest I came was pancakes with my grandma. I'm lucky if I get one meaningful word out of my mom."

Mindy yawned. "I guess I am lucky."

She stretched and rolled over onto Manson. Her breasts pressed against his stomach and her chin rested on his chest. Her big eyes stared into his as the warmness of her torso enveloped him.

He ran his hands through her hair and kissed her forehead. "How did I get so lucky?"

"You tell me."

They smiled.

"I should be leaving, shouldn't I?"

"It is getting late. The parents might be getting a bit suspicious."

"All right." Manson sighed. "I guess if I have to."

"I can give you a ride." Mindy rolled over onto her back.

"It's all right. I'm in the mood for a late-night walk." Manson stood up, stretching his arms toward the ceiling and yawning.

"Are you going home?"

"No, back to the shack."

"You have to face your family eventually."

"Eventually …" He leaned in for a goodbye kiss. "I love you."

"I love you too."

Manson slipped out of the room silently. The soft glow of the living room shone behind him as he sneaked out the door. He gently shut it, leaving the warmth of the apartment behind. The quietness of the moment was suddenly interrupted by Richard's loud voice.

"Leaving without a goodbye?" He leaned against the balcony railing that overlooked the parking lot. Smoke escaped his mouth as he spoke, becoming one with the dark night. The cigar clutched in his fingers simmered smoothly as he observed Manson.

"I guess I … just didn't want to interrupt you guys."

Manson's white lie caused Richard an amused smirk. "I'm glad I'm able to talk to you one on one." Richard puffed on his cigar. Manson shifted nervously. "Felicia and I have noticed a change in Mindy lately. I think we know why now."

"A good change?" Manson asked in a tone that was desperate to be casual.

"Definitely good. *You're* good for her, Manson. Mindy has been happier since meeting you."

"I'm glad," Manson confidently said. "I care about her … I really do. I want you to know that."

"I'm glad." Richard mimicked Manson's statement as he knocked ash off his cigar. "You should know, Manson … Mindy is a fragile girl. Tip her too far in one direction, and she may break." Richard threw the end of the cigar into the parking lot. "Be careful with my daughter."

The statement wasn't intimidating, which made its meaning even more abstract. Richard nodded a goodbye and walked inside. Manson was left to contemplate the conversation as the night consumed him.

INTERLUDE

I could taste the ash in his mouth as we clung to each other in the shower. The cigarettes he'd smoked lay on his tongue. Thousands of inhales and exhales have left his lips tainted and his lungs tired. There's something beautiful about that—the persistent habit of addiction clinging to his soul like an infection he's consented to.

I admire that kind of persistence. One of the many things I admire about my man. He's dedicated to those around him. He could have done anything, been anyone, but he stayed. Stayed out of love. Love for a woman who couldn't even call him by his name. And for another woman who failed to raise him. And for a brother who forgot him to the past. He may not think he loves them, but I can see it in his eyes. He hates them too much to not love them. In the end, the people we love have the ability to hurt us. And out of hurt comes hate.

Is that what I'll do to the ones who love me? Will I hurt them like I hurt myself? That is my biggest fear and a reality I have come to terms with. I've already hurt them. Worse than I could ever hurt myself. I catch my mother glancing at my wrists. Hurt gleams in the corner of her eye, but she shoves it back, like the strong woman she is. I'm sorry I'm not strong like you. I'm sorry.

Will I hurt you, Manson? If I do, I'm sorry. I don't mean to. I mean to love you. But love leads to hurt. And hurt to hate. Don't hate me, Manson. I couldn't bear that. Just love me, Manson. Hold me tight under running water, and let me out of my flesh for a while. Let me breathe without these dark thoughts, at least for a moment. Let me feel you feeling me, and let me forget who I am. Just for a moment.

—Mindy
(Journal Entry)

Life is a distraction
From death's infatuation,
With the narrative presentation
Of the dreaded ending.

—Mindy

ELEVEN

Mindy stared down at the pill resting in her palm. The blue capsule embodied the hate she felt toward what her life was becoming. She looked up lazily into the mirror. Her eyes were glossed over. They looked like they belonged somewhere else.

A knock came from outside the bathroom door. "Are you doing okay, hon?"

"Yeah, Mom." Mindy's lips moved, but she didn't feel like she was talking.

"Just making sure. Make sure you take your pills.

"Yes, Mom."

Mindy looked down again. She had to remind herself that it was better this way. She didn't feel like dying anymore. In fact, she barely felt anything anymore. She looked up again.

Apparently feeling nothing was better than being dead. She popped the pill, settling into her numbness.

It was a sunny day, a perfect day for the annual Gatford Fair. Mindy always thought calling it a *fair* was generous. There was one bouncy house, two or three games, and a single food cart. Granted, the local businesses took the opportunity to lure customers in with unbeatable deals. Felicia left Mindy with her brother while she went chasing bargains.

Mindy sat outside the bouncy house, a large pair of sunglasses covering her eyes. Her brother was inside, terrorizing other children with his inhuman ability to bounce higher than them. Mindy clutched an uneaten ice cream cone. It had melted, and its cool white stickiness dripped down the cone and through her fingers. It hit the green grass with a splat. Ants congregated around the mess of liquid. Mindy watched them.

She thought that maybe they were trying to pick up the melted mess. If they were, it wasn't working. Each one of them drowned in the sugary slime. Yet they continued trying. It reminded Mindy of humans. How often did people repeat the same behavior, expecting different results? How often did she? She chuckled, realizing how emo her thought process was. She was self-aware enough to notice the problem, which made the fact that she couldn't change it that much worse.

Her eyes flickered about the small fair. Maybe Manson would be there. She knew he wouldn't, but she hoped anyway. He was still at the shack. She had tried to convince him to go home, but he wasn't ready. She understood that. He kept sneaking into her apartment to take showers, usually during the day or before work, while the parents were gone.

The two of them would stand under the hot water, their lips locked and their hands wrapped around each other's naked torsos. Mindy loved the way he felt her. She had never had something like that. It made her happy. But like everything else that made her happy, she dreaded losing it.

"Mindy!" her brother shrieked. "Look how high I'm bouncing!"

"Nice job, buddy," Mindy said. She cast her eyes back down to the ants. There was a pile of them mixed in with the ice cream.

"Mindy!" It was Felicia this time. She walked up, a napkin in hand. "You got ice cream all over yourself!" She grabbed the cone from Mindy's grasp and wiped her sticky hands clean. "Are you okay?"

Felicia looked at Mindy the way she always did. Mindy hated it. She knew what her mom really wanted to ask. *Are you still depressed? Why are you sad? Am I doing something wrong?*

"I'm fine, Mom. Thanks."

"It's okay if you're not, honey. I love you either way."

She said that all the time. Mindy felt guilty for being irritated at the comment. She sighed loudly and instantly wished she hadn't. Her mom caught it, and despite her best attempts to hide her hurt, Mindy could see the wounded look in her eye. Mindy hated herself for what she did to the people around her.

"I bought you some stuff for college." Felicia did her best to press on with the conversation. She reached into the bags she had with her.

College. Mindy hadn't been thinking about that as much as she should have. It was less and less of a distant event and more and more of an ever-present reality.

"I got you this cute skirt." Felicia held out the flowery red piece of clothing. "You'll drive the college boys crazy with this."

"I hope by *college boys* you mean Manson." The irritation was apparent in Mindy's voice.

"Honey, I didn't mean—"

"You don't think we're going to last, do you?" Mindy could feel herself getting worked up.

"Don't be so rash! You know how I can run my mouth sometimes. I didn't—"

"I'm going to walk home. I'll see you later."

"Mindy …" Felicia's feeble attempts to keep her daughter by her side were useless. She was already gone, walking away with her arms crossed.

When Mindy got home, she collapsed onto her bed and pulled out her journal. She began writing.

> When no one believes, are you the one who's deceived?

She tapped the end of her pen against the bottom of her lip. She contemplated the next verse.

> Or are they wrong? And you're the one who's strong?

She got bored and began writing something else.

> Like ants, we march forward, instinctively self-destructing with each step. And with each breath we take, we fake the idea that we can see what really matters. It's all a repeating pattern, a futile …

Mindy threw her pen aside. She ran her fingers through her hair. She wrestled with the familiar temptation to reach under her bed. She hid a secret there. She reached out, touching the knife blade she hid under her pillow. She gently rubbed her thumb against the sharp edge. Her heart began beating faster. She drew her hand away, aware that she needed a distraction.

She texted Manson, "All right if I come over?"

A few seconds later, he responded, "Nothing would make me happier."

Mindy jumped off her bed, glad to leave the empty apartment behind.

Why do we fight tears?
They well in our eyes,
Trying to tell us something.
But we silence them.
We hide behind steely masks and empty personas.
And we hide the cry of our minds.

—Mindy

TWELVE

Manson didn't know what to feel as his brother pulled out of the driveway. Dan's warmth still lingered from their hug. His brother was off to start a new life, and Manson was still in Gatford.

Dan waved one last time as he rounded the corner. "I'll call," he shouted as his car disappeared into the distance.

Mother walked inside, but Manson stayed, staring into the distance. Soon night fell and he was left standing in the cold, lonely dark.

A month passed with no phone call. Then two, then three. It wasn't until the fourth month that Manson's heart grew bitter. He started working at the gas station after Mother lost her factory job. As he stood behind the register day after day, his soul grew hard. He no longer bothered cutting his hair or washing the smell of cigarettes off his clothes.

"Dan called today." It was month six.

"What did he say?" Manson asked, trying to hide the hint of excitement that his soul indulged in.

Mother inhaled. She'd started smoking inside. Grandma was too frail to stop her. "Not much. Just that things are going well."

"Oh." The excitement withered. "Okay."

Over those six months, Manson got acceptance letter after acceptance letter to colleges that spanned states and even countries. He threw them in the trash.

"Dan!"

"It's Manson, Grandma."

"Oh, I'm sorry, honey. These old eyes are starting to play tricks on me."

As the months wore on, Manson stopped insisting that Grandma call him by his name. It was a fight he was destined to lose.

"Dan called today."

It had been a year.

"Did he talk to Grandma?"

"No, we didn't talk very long."

All Manson could feel was anger. Every repetition of Dan's name that slipped from his grandmother's lips forced him deeper into that rage.

"Dan called today."

It had been a year and a half.

"I don't care."

Mom stopped telling Manson when Dan called, on the rare occasion that he did.

Soon two years had passed by. Manson stood dull eyed behind the register, yawning loudly.

"Hey, I'm the new trainee."

Manson barely heard the words as he zoned back into reality. He slowly turned his head. "Don't get too excited. This job's pretty—" Manson halted midsentence. His mouth hung open slightly as butterflies danced through his stomach.

"Pretty what?" Mindy asked.

"Oh, sorry. It can be pretty boring."

"I can do boring."

Her smile infected Manson's soul.

Dan hated being stuck in the small town of Gatford. He hated being stuck in a house polluted with smoke and the smell of tobacco. He grew to resent his mother. She sat endlessly in front of the TV, burning her life away, along with the cigarettes she smoked.

He occupied his days with working out. He jogged around town like a caged rat running on an endlessly spinning wheel. He was counting down the days until his grandmother's funeral. He hated himself for it.

He thought about his brother a lot. It had been about a week since their last confrontation. He played it over and over in his mind. The man he had argued with held no resemblance to the boy he had left behind three years ago. He tried to envision the transformation that must have taken place, but as much as he tried, he couldn't visualize it.

Dan walked into the house, sweaty from a jog. Smoke wafted past him, escaping the confines of the house and reaching up like deformed fingers toward the sky. "You should really open a window, Mom."

"Go ahead and open one."

Dan walked into the kitchen, throwing the blinds back.

"There's a glare on my TV!"

Dan ignored her and opened the window, letting fresh air into the house. Dan suddenly noticed a cop car sliding to a stop in the driveway. Two officers stepped out and approached the house. Dan answered the door as the bell rang.

"Hello, Officers, how may I help you?" Dan put on his polite military voice. His mother peeked her head around to see what was happening.

"Is Manson here?" The officer's voice was harsh and uncaring.

"No, sir. I haven't seen him in about a week. I'm Dan, his brother." He reached out his hand politely, but the officers ignored it.

"Do you have any idea where he might be?"

Dan turned toward his mother. She shook her head.

"What's this all about?" Dan asked.

The officers handed Dan a piece of paper. He was confused as he looked down and saw a badly drawn penis with the words *suck on this* written below it.

"We arrested a man named Dex for throwing a brick through a window with this message on it." Dan looked up. "He was also charged with vandalism for spray-painting a similar image on the side of a house. There were reports that he had two accomplices. We believe your brother was one of them."

Dan handed the slip of paper back. "What makes you think that?" Dan's skeptical eyes looked the officers up and down. They straightened up, doing their best to look intimidating. Dan saw through them.

"We'd just like to ask him a few questions."

"Do you actually *know* if he was involved in any way?"

"We know that he has been involved with this individual on prior occasions, leading us to believe that—"

"I see," Dan said with a certain level of arrogance. "You're saying my brother is guilty by association?"

"Sir, we just want—"

"Next time you stop by, make sure to bring a warrant, not a shitty drawing of a dick." Dan slammed the door. He ran to the window and shut it, closing the blinds as well. He watched to make sure the officers left.

"You always did look out for your brother, didn't you?"

Dan passively listened to his mother as he put his shoes on. "I'll be back."

His mother said nothing as he stepped out the door.

Dan sat outside the gas station. His car was parked in the back of the parking lot. He hadn't seen Manson come out for a smoke break once, leading him to believe Manson wasn't at work. He could just walk in, but he didn't want to risk it.

He smoked a cigar. His hand hung casually out the window, the cigar held between his index and middle finger. The smoke wafted through the warm summer day, simmering in the hot air. The afternoon drifted into evening, and his cigar disappeared into ash.

The young black girl eventually wandered outside and into her car. She had a picnic basket. She drove off, and Dan followed her, careful not to arouse suspicion. Part of him was uncomfortable with what he was doing, but he had to find his brother, and this girl was the only lead he had.

The farther into the country they drove, the farther behind her Dan trailed. She became a dot in the distance that he had to keep track of. Eventually, she led him down a dirt road. In order to stay unnoticed, he pulled over and parked next to some bushes. He got out and walked.

The sun beat down on him, causing sweat to pour out of every orifice. The dirt and pebbles crunched beneath his feat. He reached the end of the road. He saw the girl's car parked down a grassy path. He slipped into the forest. He was too deep in thought to admire the bright green leaves that caught the sunlight in just the right way. Grass tugged half-heartedly at his ankles. He heard voices in the distance. He recognized his brother's deep snarl.

The forest cleared, revealing a run-down shack and an old rusted car. Manson and his girlfriend sat on a blanket, feeding each other out of a picnic basket. The sun illuminated them in an almost divine way. Manson looked ragged and grungy, while the girl looked cute and clean, like a blooming flower. It was a pristine scene full of contradictions. Dan felt almost bad for interrupting it.

He stepped out of the shadows. Mindy jumped in surprise. Manson's eyes were drawn to his brother. He quickly stood up. "What are you doing here? How did you find me?"

"Who is this?" Mindy asked, perplexed, glancing between Manson and Dan with concern. She stood up, standing by Manson's side.

"I'm Dan." He stepped forward, his hand outstretched. "Manson's brother."

Mindy looked at Manson, as if asking permission to shake Dan's hand. Manson glared at his brother with an equal amount of frustration and confusion. "What is this?" he asked.

"I'm concerned about you." Dan lowered his hand. "I haven't seen you in days, and today the police came looking for you. What's going on, man?"

Manson looked pissed. "Last time I saw you I punched you. And now you're telling me you're *concerned*?"

"We're brothers, aren't we?"

Dan's question was followed by silence. Manson turned toward Mindy. "Would you mind letting us talk alone for a bit?"

"Sure." She kissed Manson on the cheek and slid into the shack.

"I don't forgive you," Manson sneered.

"For what?" Dan sighed. At this point he was prepared for Manson's dickish comments.

"For everything. For leaving me here."

"I don't care if you forgive me. We're brothers, and you need to get over it."

"Get over it!" Manson began. "Why don't you—"

"We're not doing this again!" Dan cut in. "I'm not arguing with you! You need to come home!"

"Don't tell me what I need."

"You sound like a fucking child, Manson!" Dan was yelling now. "The fucking cops showed up asking about you! This isn't like when we were kids! You can't hide here forever!"

"Not forever, just till this blows over. I'll come home when it's safe."

"Till what blows over?" Dan pressed. "What did you do?"

"It doesn't concern you."

Dan laughed in disbelief. "You weren't always like this, Manson. What happened?"

"Three fucking years happened!"

"I fucked up, okay?" Dan pounded his chest, his hands emoting on their own. "I should have called; I should have visited! What the fuck do you want me to do about it?"

"I want you to leave." Manson's words were cutting. "I want you to disappear like you did three years ago. Except this time … stay gone."

Dan was astonished by the vitriol his brother spewed. "That's what you really want?"

"Yes." Manson was clear in his demand.

"Why do you hate me so much?" Dan asked earnestly. "Why do you resent me?"

Manson flashed back to his grandma saying Dan's name. He held his rage down. He let it burn inside of him, and he hid it. As much as he resented his brother, he didn't want him to know. "You promised you'd be there for me." Manson's eyes brimmed with tears. "When we were kids, you said you'd always be there for me. You lied."

"I said I'm sorry," Dan quietly said.

"Don't be. Just realize that things can never be the same." Manson walked away, disappearing into the shack like a shadow.

Dan walked back up the dirt road, his shirt heavy with sweat and his heart heavy with contemplation. He drove away, smoking yet another cigar. He didn't go home; instead, he stopped by the railroad tracks. He parked on the side of the road and followed the rails on foot. Smoke wafted out of his mouth and trailed behind him.

After all these years, he still remembered the path. He remembered walking it with his brother. They'd grab a snack from the gas station and let the tracks guide them. They'd dodge oncoming trains and watch from the forest as they passed. It was all they had to do in a town of no opportunities.

Dan found the path through the forest. It had been overtaken by vegetation. He kicked the vines aside and stomped over the bushes. He reached the cliff face and looked over the trees and the distant town. It was just like he remembered. He was glad that at least this hadn't changed. He tossed his cigar over the edge and sat down, letting the sun set as tears welled in his eyes. He didn't hold them back.

INTERLUDE

"Faggot!"

"At least my neck isn't the size of a fucking blimp, you Cabbage Patch–looking fuck!"

Manson laughed at Dex's poetically worded insult. The kid who had yelled the slur kept walking, looking angry. Dex and Manson sat on the ground, their backs to a line of lockers. The school moved around them. Students stood in circles, gossiping, while others walked on by, their backpacks bouncing with every step.

A toothpick hung out the side of Dex's mouth. "I hate this place."

"It's not all that bad."

"Says the straight-A student."

Manson shrugged. "Schoolwork just comes easy to me."

Dex dramatically flung his head against the back of the locker, a tinny echo reverberating through the chamber. "I wish I were high."

"We smoked a joint this morning."

"It wasn't enough."

"Your tolerance is getting way too high, bro."

"I know." Dex sighed. "I miss the days when I could get baked off one hit."

The bell rang. They stood up, heading for class.

Dex was late. They always met outside the school, ten minutes after the last bell rang. It had been twenty minutes. Now thirty. Manson was prepared to walk back into the building when he saw his friend limping around the side of the school. His eyes were blackened, and his body bloody and bruised.

"Dude!" Manson ran up, clutching Dex's shoulders. "What happened?"

"That kid ..." Dex coughed, his voice weak. "The one who called me a faggot ..."

Rage filled Manson. "He did this to you?"

"Him and his friends."

Manson's eyes swiveled around. "It's okay. We'll get those fuckers back."

"Come on, man. I know you know where they hang out!" Manson walked in step with his brother, trying to keep up with his massive stride.

"I don't." Dan was jogging around town. His brother's presence was slowing him down to a crawl.

"You're on the football team with them! You have to know!"

Dan stared ahead, ignoring his brother. Manson leaped in front of him, blocking his path. Dan tried going around, but Manson dogged left and right, keeping him in his place. Dan gave up, looking down at his brother.

"Why do you want to know?"

"They beat the shit outta Dex."

Dan's brow furrowed. "Are you sure?"

"Of course I'm fucking sure!"

Dan's lips pressed into a hard line, causing an odd expression. "What are you planning?"

Manson didn't answer.

Dan sighed. "There's an old shack outside of town. They hang out there and smoke weed. Whatever you're planning ..." Dan paused. "Don't get caught, don't drag me into it, and make sure it works."

He jogged on, leaving his brother behind.

It was the dead of night. Dex and Manson crouched outside the shack. They could hear the three boys inside, laughing and talking about girls they'd supposedly banged. Dex and Manson held baseball bats. They looked at each other.

"Are you ready for this?" Manson whispered.

Dex nodded. "Let's fuck up these assholes."

With a violent kick, Manson flung the door open. Pot smoke wafted out as the boys looked over in surprise. Manson brought his bat down, smashing the bong that sat on the floor. The glass shattered violently, shards sliding across the wood floor.

"What the fu—" one of the boys began as Dex smashed him in the face. Blood cascaded out his nose as the back of his head slammed against the ground.

"Bro, my fucking bong!" The boy with the big neck stood up, his eyes a deep red.

"Call me a faggot now, motherfucker!" Dex slammed his bat into the boy's stomach. He joined his friend on the floor. The third boy bolted out the door and into the night.

"Get up! Get the fuck up!"

They prodded the two boys outside, slamming them onto the ground. The boy with the large neck cradled his stomach as he stood up. Blood covered his teeth. The other boy held his nose, trying to stop the flow of blood.

"Now listen the fuck up!" Manson pointed his bat at the boys. "This shack is ours now, got that? We ever see you here, we'll fuck you up! You tell anyone about this, we'll fuck you up. You even look at us wrong in school, we'll fuck you up. You touch my friend ever again, I will end your fucking life!"

"This isn't over!" the big-necked boy threatened.

"It's *not*?" Dex swung at the boy's face. He fell backward and hit the ground hard. "Tell me when you want it to be over, motherfucker!" Dex swung repeatedly. Manson watched the other boy, making sure he didn't run for it.

"I want it to be over!"

"Of course you do, pussy-ass bitch!" Dex gave the boy one last, hard kick. "Now stand the fuck up!" He did as he was told. "I never want to see your Cabbage Patch–looking ass around me ever again! Stay the fuck away from me and my friends! Got it?" The boys nodded vehemently. "And if you even think of trying to get us back for this, so help me God we'll chop your balls off and make you eat them! Now fuck off!"

The boys ran into the forest. Dex and Manson looked at each other. Their breath was heavy, and their skin was sticky with sweat.

Manson smiled. "We did it."

They hugged.

Memories burn,
And time turns,
With or without you,
Into
A new chapter.

—Mindy

THIRTEEN

Dan and Manson sat on the couch, game controllers in hand. Their characters bounced back and forth with each touch of a button. Grandma stood in the kitchen, preparing dinner. Her hands delicately pressed floury dough into a circular pan.

"You don't want to use that attack," Dan warned as his character hopped back. "It's not going to work on my guy."

"Sounds like something you'd say if you're scared of getting your ass kicked."

"Hey!" Grandma warned. "Language!"

Manson's character jumped into the air, coming down toward Dan, who easily blocked and countered. Manson's character flew to the edge of the screen, a stream of pixelated blood following. The big red word DEATH flashed across the screen as Manson's character exploded into pieces.

"Come on!" Manson exclaimed, throwing the controller onto his lap. "This is bullshit!"

"Hey!" Grandma searched through the freezer, pulling out a large Ziploc bag. "What did I just say! Aunt Mary is visiting tonight, and I do not want you acting this way."

Both Dan's and Manson's eyes shot over to their grandma. She turned away from the freezer, seeing the two of them gazing at her in disbelief. Her brow furrowed in confusion.

"Why are you two looking at me?"

"Grandma," Dan said somberly, "Aunt Mary's been dead for five years."

Grandma paused, confusion deepening in her eyes. "Oh." Her eyes glazed over, as if searching for a distant truth. "I knew that." She snapped out of it, throwing the Ziploc bag onto the counter and continuing with her cooking. Dan and Manson looked at each other, concern burning in their eyes.

"What did you guys talk about?" Mindy asked.

Manson sighed heavily. "I don't even know," he admitted.

They were curled up together on the old couch. The daylight had faded but they had an old-fashioned gas lamp to give light. It cast long shadows over the wood planks as it flickered continually, avoiding the gaze of the lovers.

"When I talk to him," Manson continued, "it's like I disappear. Anger overtakes me."

Mindy nuzzled up closer to him. They lay beneath a large blue blanket. Mindy's eyes drifted lazily with sleep. Manson, however, was wide awake. He stared relentlessly at the flickering flame, deep in thought.

"You have a right to be angry." Mindy yawned. "From everything you've told me, he sounds like a dick."

"Every time I see him," Manson droned on, the fire reflected in his eyes, "I hear my grandma saying his name."

Mindy twisted herself around until she was facing him. "I'm sorry." The shadows danced around her face in a way that made her look like a dream.

Manson half expected to wake up, hearing his grandma calling. "The worst part is … I remember when I loved him," he said as he rolled his fingers through Mindy's curly locks. Her black hair was like ash in the dark. Manson kissed her on the forehead. She crinkled her nose and closed her eyes. She nuzzled her head against his chest.

"I leave in a month." She said it so quietly it almost didn't sound like a bad thing.

"For college?"

"What else?" She hugged Manson tight beneath the sheets. "What's going to happen to us?"

Manson was not prepared for that question. "What do you want to happen?"

"I don't want it to end." She burrowed even deeper against Manson's chest.

"Me neither." Manson caressed her beneath the sheets.

There was a sudden banging at the door. Mindy jumped. Manson threw the blanket aside. "Who's there?" He thrust Mindy off him gently and stood up.

"Who do you think, numb-nuts?" Dex kicked the door open. He wore a wide smile and held several bags. He looked disheveled and deranged.

"Dex!" Manson sprang toward his friend. "I thought they caught you, dude!"

"They did." Dex set the bags down, smiling. "But I got my cousin to post bail."

The two of them hugged.

"We're sorry for leaving you," Mindy apologized. "I wish we could have done something."

"There was no point in all of us getting caught," Dex reassured her. "I'm glad you guys are happy to see me, but it's not all good news and celebration."

Manson felt a dread build in his gut. "You're going on the run, aren't you?"

"Not exactly." He stepped back, his smile wavering a little. "I'm just heading out to Colorado a little early. I'll lay low there."

Manson hugged Dex again. "I don't want you to leave, man."

"Don't get sappy on me." Dex pushed Manson away playfully. "I didn't come back to cry and share our feelings. I came back to fucking party!" Dex reached into one of the bags and pulled out a six-pack of beer and a bottle of liquor.

They spent the night smoking and drinking. They reminisced on times past. Mindy enjoyed the stories that poured from their lips. Every conversation seemed to begin with "Remember that time ..." and end with laughter.

"Remember when we found that piece of shit?" Dex nodded lazily at the couch. At this point, their eyes were glazed over. They sat in a circle around the lamp, which burned with less and less vigor as the night wore on.

"It was off the side of the highway, wasn't it?" Manson took a hit and then passed the blunt to Mindy.

"Yeah ..." Dex swayed back and forth lazily. His eyes were red and unfocused. "Let's burn it!" he shouted enthusiastically.

"What?" Mindy giggled, passing the blunt back.

"Let's burn this whole damn place to the ground!" Dex motioned sporadically, spilling vodka on the floor.

"Why?" Manson asked, smoke rolling out of his mouth.

"As a last hurrah!" Dex raised both his hands in victory, spilling even more vodka. "As a final fuck-you to this shitty town!"

Manson laughed. "You're wasted, dude."

"That's when I get my best ideas." Dex stood up, grabbing the lantern. "Get ready to run!"

"Fuck." Manson swore in acceptance. He stood up and ushered Mindy out the door. Dex threw the lantern at the couch. It burst into flames violently. Dex ran for the door, laughing hysterically the whole time.

"Burn, you asshole!" he shouted. He somehow managed to grab the bags of alcohol on his way out.

Outside, Mindy and Manson sat far away from the shack, their backs against a tree. Dex plopped down next to them, setting the bags down.

Flames crawled up the shack like fingers. The fingers closed into a fist, engulfing the night air. They could feel the heat emanating toward them like hot breath from a warm kiss. They watched it burn as they drank their fill. Manson thought of all the memories he had attached to that stupid little shack. He fell deeper into a drunken state as he watched his memories burn.

Everything is left unfinished.
There is no book-ending.
Just a continual move forward,
Until we collapse into the ground,
Our souls not making a sound,
As they depart from our filthy skin.

—Mindy

FOURTEEN

The Humvees marched lazily down the desert landscape. Dust trailed behind them. Dan stared calmly out the back-seat window; the hilly landscape looked back with no emotion. The helmet that rested on his head weighed down his scalp, but he'd become accustomed to the constant pressure.

"Hey," Thad said, sitting next to Dan. "No need to look so grim."

"We're crossing through enemy territory," Dan replied. "You'd do well to remember that."

Thad smiled. "Always the realist, aren't you?"

"Quiet down back there!" a stern voice commanded from up front. "This isn't a social event. Do I need to remind you of that, Thad?"

"No, sir," Thad replied. His voice became more formal, but his demeanor remained relaxed and cocky. "Dan was just reminding me of the same—"

Thad's remark remained unfinished. A thunderous explosion boomed out from beneath

133

the truck. Before anyone had time to process what had happened, the truck was flipped upside down. Dan's vision came in and out of focus as he hung upside down, the seatbelt keeping him from falling.

"Thad?" he called out, as the sound of bullets filled the air. He looked over to see his comrade, lifeless. A piece of shrapnel had penetrated his skull, leaving his face a bloody lump.

Dan unbuckled himself, falling onto the ceiling with a loud thump. He did the same to Thad, whose body fell like a rag doll into his hands. He dragged the corpse out of the shattered window, shards of glass digging into his uniform.

"What are you doing, soldier?" The sergeant had made it out and was crouching, using the flipped car as cover. Bullets sprayed into the car's side, infecting the air with death.

"Saving … I'm saving—"

"He'd dead!" The sergeant stood up, firing a few shots before crouching back down. "Now get up and fi—"

A bullet pierced the sergeant's skull, spraying blood onto Dan's face. As he blinked the brain matter out of his eyes, he saw fighters coming from behind a hill in the distance. He lay behind Thad's body as bullets pierced the corpse. Dan reached out, grabbing the gun from the sergeant's limp hands.

He shot. A miss. Another shot. One down. Then two. Then three. Friendly fire came from the Humvees behind him. Soon the desert landscape was stained with blood and bodies.

"Get up, soldier!" The second in command (now the first) ran up to Dan once the firefight had died down.

"But the bodies!"

"We'll send a crew to retrieve them. On your feet!"

"But—"

"Up *now*, soldier!"

Dan followed orders, jumping to his feet and following the second in command to a nearby vehicle. He looked back at the corpses. Thad's disfigured face would haunt his dreams from that day forward.

By the time Dan got back to the car, it was dark outside. He wiped his teary cheeks clean. He tried to remember the last time he had cried like that. Probably not since he was a child. The only time he had allowed himself to cry in the military was when he was injured. He had spent a lot of time trying to forget those injuries, but in his moment of weakness, he felt a sting of remembrance.

He sat in the car, and before long, his fingers subconsciously clutched his thigh. There was a scar there about three inches long. A knife wound. He could almost feel the blade ripping his flesh. Another flashback, this time of a shoulder wound. A bullet had pierced him there, and the pain had almost knocked him out. He shook the memories away, refusing to let himself feel the pain. If there was one thing he had learned in the military, it was that the less you thought, the less you hurt.

He drove around the back roads for a bit. He refused to go home. He envisioned his mother sitting there, smoking her life away. He suddenly wondered how she afforded it. *Manson must buy cigarettes for her*, he concluded. The thought made him sick and bitter.

He contemplated going back to the shack, trying to make things right one more time. But he knew it was pointless. He continued driving, not noticing the billowing smoke that came from deep within the forest. Eventually, Dan found his way back into town. The local bar was still open. The glowing lights and festive music drew him in.

He found himself sipping a beer and staring down at the counter. He sat silently on a bar stool while chatter surrounded him. People smoked outside the open doorway, while young men played pool and emphatically exclaimed remarks.

Why am I here? he wondered. He got up to leave but suddenly heard someone call his name. He looked over at a pool table. "Mark?"

A tall, handsome man smiled at him "Sure is, man." They embraced in a brotherly hug. "I haven't seen you since graduation!" Mark stepped back, looking Dan up and down. "Damn, you bulked up!"

Dan smiled. "The military will do that to you."

"Wanna play a game?" Mark motioned at the table.

"Sure! My skills may be a bit rusty, but I'll give it a whirl."

Mark set up the table while Dan grabbed a stick.

"So, three years into the military"—Mark carefully lifted the triangular rack—"how you enjoying it?"

"Well …" Dan lined up his shot. "I don't know if I'd use the word *enjoy*." He expertly broke the triangle, sending balls flying in every direction. "But I'm glad I joined. It's given me a sense of purpose. What about you? What have you been up to since graduation?"

"College." Mark gazed at the table, looking for a good shot. "One more year, and I'll be a certified therapist."

"Therapist? What made you want to do that?"

"Same thing that made you join the military." Mark made his shot. "A sense of purpose."

"Hmm …" Dan sipped his beer before approaching the table. "Different strokes, I guess."

"Yeah." Mark watched Dan, trying to decide if he should ask the question he'd been contemplating. "If you don't mind my asking, have you ever …" He hesitated.

"Killed anybody?" Dan leaned over the table, positioning his pool stick.

"I'm sorry. That's probably not appropriate to ask."

"It's fine." Dan straightened up as the clatter of balls filled the room. "I've been shot at, and I've shot at others. I'll leave it at that."

"Sorry if that was intrusive." Mark accidentally hit the eight ball in, losing the game.

"It's fine," Dan repeated as he sat back on a bar stool.

"What brings you to town anyway?"

"A funeral."

"I'm sorry for your loss." Mark motioned at the bartender. "Another beer, please."

"Thanks." Dan took a long swig. "It was my grandma."

"That must be hard for you."

"She was old. It was bound to happen sooner or later." Dan sighed deeply. "What about you? Why are you in town?"

"Well, it's not nostalgia, I can promise you that." Mark's statement dripped with sarcasm. "I was glad to leave this dump."

"I feel ya. I hate being stuck here." Dan was happy to find someone who could relate. "I would have left sooner if there hadn't been … complications."

"Complications?"

"Money issues," Dan admitted. "My mom's on government assistance. Paying for the funeral turned out to be complicated. I've had to fill out so much fucking paperwork for her, not to mention diving into my own pocket."

"Well, it's nice of you to take on that burden for her."

Dan looked longingly at the doorway. "I guess you could say it's a habit."

"Not the worst habit, I guess." Mark turned away to grab his beer. "Hey, you know, I'm not certified yet, but if you ever want to rant to someone, feel free—" Mark turned back to see that Dan had left. Out of the corner of his eye, he saw the silhouette of his friend exiting the building. His half-empty beer bottle sat unfinished.

INTERLUDE

Mom has started standing over me when I take my pills to make sure I'm actually taking them, of course. Like the shadow of all the guilt that eats at me. The guilt of who I actually am. The sad girl hiding behind smiles that should be genuine.

I should be happy. I have more than most. A place to sleep, a family that loves me, a boyfriend I care for more than I can explain. And yet here I am. A frown hidden behind glistening white teeth. Teeth spending their days spreading lies as they gnaw themselves into oblivion. They should be gray and rotted. Ugly, like me. My skin should be shriveled and my eyes weak and weary. But instead, I stand with fair skin and lively eyes that fool those around me into loving me.

Don't love me. It makes everything so much harder. To know that who I am behind glistening white teeth will one day hurt those I love is too much to live with. I'd rather not live with that. Or live at all.

There I go again. Being honest. Honesty is why I have to hide this journal under my mattress. If my mother were to read this, she'd know the ugly me. She'd try to make me pretty. But ugly is who I am. You can hide yourself from others, but you can't hide

138

behind your own teeth. They scream at you from within, sinking into your soul and bleeding your heart dry.

Let me bleed. Dry me up, and lay me down. When I go six feet under, don't give me a gravestone. Leave the dirt to eat me, and don't remember who I was. Put my writings down there with me so no reminders are left in my wake. Just my writings and me forever, alone with the dirt and the worms.

—Mindy
(Journal Entry)

Ash falls like snow.
I ask for your love,
Afraid you'll say no.
But you say yes,
And on we go,
To the ash-covered ground,
Full of the past you know.

—Mindy

FIFTEEN

Mindy scraped the knife blade against her shoulder. There wasn't as much blood as the wrist, but it was something. And this way, no one would know. A small stream of blood escaped from the incision, caressing her arm as it slowly dripped. Something about the slow trickle calmed her. It was like watching a red waterfall in slow motion. A waterfall made up of small pieces of her.

A sudden knock at the door. Mindy's eyes snapped away from the mirror.

"I have some freshly laundered towels," Felicia announced as she barged in.

"No, Mom!" But it was too late.

Felicia dropped the towels as she looked over Mindy's naked torso. Blood had reached her elbow, dripping onto the tile floor. "No," Felicia whispered. "No, no, no …"

"Mom, just—"

"I thought we were over this!" Tears welled in Felicia's eyes. "The pills, the therapist!" She clapped her hands over her face.

"It was an accident—I swear!"

"Don't lie!" Felicia yelled. "Don't lie to me!"

"I'm sorry." It was Mindy's turn to have teary eyes. "I'm sorry. I—"

"What's going on in here?" Richard burst in, the door swinging wide open. "Oh, my God …"

"What's going on?" Mindy's little brother called out, bouncing down the hallway.

"No!" Richard grabbed him, pulling him back down the hallway. "Let's play some video games."

"I'm sorry." Mindy's face contorted as tears welled in her eyes, and her cheeks grew moist. "I'm sorry."

Felicia put on a strong face as she wiped her daughter's arm. "Let's get you cleaned up. Let's start a hot bath for you. I'll be here the whole time, okay? I'll be here."

Later that night, Mindy had to watch as her parents tore her room apart, looking for anything she could use to hurt herself. She glanced at the fresh bandage covering her shoulder. The next day she skipped school and went straight to the therapist. Her parents sat right next to her. She gazed at the floor.

When Mindy woke up, her head was pounding. She burrowed into Manson's chest, desperately trying to hide from the outside world. When she finally did open her eyes, she was blinded by harsh light. She sat back for a while, letting her head pound like a drumbeat. The world slowly but surely came into focus.

They were lying inside the old car. She didn't remember how they got there. It had to be around midday. She sat for an hour, letting the hangover play itself out. Eventually, her eyes wandered over to the remains of the shack. Charred planks of wood lay on the ash-ridden floor. She sighed. She didn't remember much of the night before, but the image of the burning building had stayed with her. A note was taped to the windshield. Mindy red the scrawled writing.

> I had to leave. My cousin picked me up. We're on our way to Colorado by now.
>
> Manson, you are the best bro I've ever had. You're pretty cool too, Mindy.
>
> Treat my man well. I'll get in contact when I can. Peace.

Mindy looked over at Manson. Hair covered his face, and his arms were sprawled out in odd directions. As silently as she could, Mindy stepped out of the car. She kicked the empty beer bottles mindlessly as she walked about. Night wind had blown ash onto the lawn, like the rotten innards of a corpse strewn about. She walked into the skeletal remains of the shack. She felt like she was standing inside a dead creature.

"What are you doing?" Manson's voice was groggy. Lazily rubbing his eyes, he watched Mindy as he held Dex's note in his hand.

"Dancing in the remains." She twirled, bringing up a flood of ash around her. Her skirt billowed and fell as the dirty black grit covered her torso. She closed her eyes and tipped her head upward, as if to stop from inhaling the ash.

Manson smirked a half smile. "You're a strange, strange girl." He sat up.

Mindy reached a hand out toward him. "A dance?"

Manson laughed. "Are you still drunk?"

"Drunk off love."

"No," Manson said in mock sternness as he stood up. "We are not going to be that corny of a couple."

"It's only corny because it's true."

Manson grabbed her hand. They twirled around gently, the ash dancing at their feet like dirty snowflakes.

"I already miss him," Manson admitted.

"When did you guys first meet?"

"Elementary school."

"Damn," Mindy exclaimed softly. "I didn't realize it had been that long.

"Yeah …" Manson momentarily seemed lost in his thoughts. "It's just like you said … back in that yard … one moment, and it all changes."

Despite their best efforts to keep it at bay, ash still danced around them and clogged their lungs. They made their way over to the skeleton of the couch. The cushions and frame had burned away but the springs remained.

"Doesn't it ever feel like …" Manson said, "well, like you said. Sometimes it feels like it's all pointless. Dex and I have been friends for most of my life. Now I don't know if I'll ever see him again."

"You still have the memories," Mindy said. "That has to mean something. Memories are what make you who you are. The scars, the sadness … they're all part of that. But they're not everything. There's the good stuff too. There's me … and you. That has to mean something."

Mindy felt odd to be the one who was consoling. She didn't know how much of what she said she actually believed, but she knew she didn't want Manson to feel how she always felt.

"Yeah," Manson said, sighing, "you're right. Thanks for that."

Mindy pressed up against Manson like she always did. "Will you miss me?"

"What do you mean?"

"When I'm gone … like Dex."

Manson wasn't sure what to say. He stood silent. The ash seemed to freeze where it floated. The whole moment was suspended as he thought.

"You don't have to be like Dex. You can stay."

"I will," Mindy reassured, "but if I didn't … would you miss me?"

"Of course!" Manson exclaimed without hesitation. "Why would you even ask that?"

"Because when I leave for college, I want to know you'll still be there for me. And how much you miss somebody"—she kissed him on the neck—"shows how much you love them."

"I'll miss you more than you'll ever know."

She pushed herself closer. "Good."

As the summer light dimmed, the two lovers continued to dance in the remains.

The sacrifices we make
Take everything out of us.
And when it comes time to lay them down,
They make a defining noise,
A thunderous sound
That rips your ears asunder,
And drags your body six feet under.

—Mindy

SIXTEEN

The hot summer sun, sitting high in a cloudless sky, beat down on Manson and Dex. They hid in the shadow of a large church on the outskirts of town. The monolithic stone structure rose to great heights, a wooden cross piercing the sky. Through the windows, they could see empty pews and a pulpit with a lifelike statue of Jesus behind it, overlooking the absent congregation. His bloody palms were pierced with large nails and his eyes looked toward the sky. Dex and Manson sat beneath a stained-glass window, the colors bleeding onto their silhouettes. Manson smoked a cigarette with his back to the wall, while Dex twiddled his thumbs, looking down at the warm pavement.

"Did we seriously have to stop by a church?" Dex asked.

"If you want to make a confession, now would be the time," Manson joked.

"I confess to hating this place." Dex leaned his head against the wall, straining his eyes to catch a glimpse of the stained-glass window.

"Aren't you the edgy teen." Manson knocked ash off his cigarette.

"It's hard not to hate things that hate you."

"We all choose our own gods, I guess," Manson said apathetically.

"What are my gods?" Dex wondered aloud.

"Weed and dick."

"Clever." There was a hint of sadness in Dex's gruff tone.

"You okay, dude?" Manson asked as smoke wafted out of his nostrils.

"I just don't like churches."

"It's just four walls and a roof, like any other building."

"That's not true." Dex glared at the shadow of the cross. "It represents hate and ignorance."

"That's not fair, man." Manson smashed the butt of his cigarette against the hot concrete. "Not everyone who is religious is ignorant and hateful."

"But they believe in something that is."

"I don't think that's true."

"You going to go religious on me, bro?"

Manson chuckled. "Naw. But I understand it. Wanting to believe there's something better after this."

Dex sighed. "Yeah, I guess that part makes sense."

"Hey!" a large man called from a side door. His handlebar mustache and bushy eyebrows were ruffled in anger. "What are you kids doing?"

Dex shrugged. "Chilling."

"What you're doing is loitering on private property! Get out of here before I call the cops."

"So much for love and tolerance," Manson quipped as he hopped on his bike.

Dex flipped the man off as they rode away, the sun beating down on their backs.

Manson walked into the house casually. His mom didn't say a thing. She didn't even ask why he was covered in ash. He threw off his clothes and quickly took a shower. Dan came home from a jog to see him smoking on the front porch.

"You're back?" he asked simply.

"Yeah."

Time drifted by aimlessly. The next few days flowed together with ease. It was all the same to Manson, who spent his time at work or with Mindy. He ignored Dan for the most part, avoiding interacting with him. The constant tension between them tore Dan apart. His wish to leave would soon be fulfilled, as the funeral fast approached. Dan made the arrangements, taking the burden off Manson's shoulders. When the day finally came, he had to motivate his mother to get up and change. She wore a plain dress with her hair tied back. Dan wore his military uniform and helped find Manson an outfit

"Are you doing okay?" Dan asked tentatively as Manson tucked in his flannel shirt.

"Why wouldn't I be?"

"We're going to our grandma's funeral." Dan tried not to say it aggressively, but the edge in his voice could not be denied.

"She died a long time ago." Manson straightened his bow tie. "All that was left of her in the end was a shell. She didn't even have most of her memories."

Dan couldn't bring himself to say anything.

They all packed into the car and rode to the funeral home. Manson sat in the back behind his mother. He looked longingly out the window.

"What's your best memory of Grandma?" Dan asked, only because he couldn't stand the morbid silence.

Their mom sighed. "She was a good mother."

Dan waited for more, but nothing came.

"Remember when she used to pack lunches for us, Manson?" Dan was grasping at straws now.

"I remember." Manson stared at his reflection in the glass as shadows of the outside world passed by.

Dan succumbed to silence and let the pretenses fall. He wanted to believe he had some semblance of a family, but that idea died as he drove into the funeral home parking lot.

Inside it was stuffy. Rows of chairs had been set up, but most of them weren't needed. A few extended relatives were spaced around the room. They all looked as if they were getting ready to join the deceased. Manson stared at the open casket as the preacher droned on. His grandmother lay motionless, her closed eyes gazing at the ceiling. Strangely, he envisioned her turning toward him, her eyelids flickering upward to reveal cold, dead eyes. *"Dan, Dan, Dan …"* She lipped the words over and over.

"And now we'll hear from Dan, Nancy's beloved grandson."

Manson was glad it was his brother speaking and not him. It's what their grandmother would have wanted.

Dan stepped up the podium, his palms cold with sweat. He looked over the room, his eyes skipping the empty seats and settling on his brother. Manson's eyes were expressionless as he looked forward blankly. He wasn't looking at Dan; he was looking past him at their grandmother.

"My grandma …" Dan began. He had spent days writing a eulogy, but in the moment, none of it seemed to matter. "My grandma … was a wonderful woman." A sharp cough from an elderly man in the back interrupted him. "She …"

The words caught in Dan's throat. He didn't know why he was nervous. He'd survived gunshots and stab wounds, but words intimidated him. The last time he had seen his grandma was three years ago. She was more than a corpse then. Dan's eyes moved back to his brother, who continued to stare at the body.

"She …" Dan stumbled over his words. "She loved Manson."

Manson snapped out of his haze. His heart skipped a beat as he realized what was happening.

Dan didn't know what he was doing, but he felt he didn't deserve to be at that podium. He was a deserter. He had left his grandmother behind, along with everything else. "Manson is the one who was with her in her last months." Dan's heart pounded. His sight was blurry from adrenaline. "He should be the one up here right now." Dan smiled as a memory popped into his head. "I remember how Grandma used to pack our lunches. She would give Manson a full-sized candy bar and me a snack-sized. That's when I knew he was her favorite." The comment was meant as a joke, but there was no laughter. "Why don't you come up here, Manson?"

Desperation rose within Manson as his brother spoke.

"Say a few words about Grandma. You knew her best."

Manson looked around awkwardly. Every eye was focused on him. Hatred overtook every bone in his body. It was an irrational hatred directed at the whole room, at the situation, at his life, but most of all at his brother. After a three-year absence, he returned, and what for? To further destroy a family that was already in ashes.

"Well … go!" Manson's mother whispered.

He awkwardly stood up, his fists clenched involuntarily. He walked up to the podium, wanting nothing more than to step away. But he remained frozen under the watchful eyes glued to him.

"It's all right; I got your back," Dan whispered. He put his hand on Manson's shoulder, who tensed up. Despite the physical touch, Dan could feel the distance between them. It was palpable.

Manson glanced around the room. Adrenaline pumped through his veins, blurring his vision. Anger pulsated beneath his skin like an infection. He turned toward his brother. "You're going to regret this."

Dan's hand fell from Manson's shoulder, and a sinking feeling enveloped his gut.

"Grandma, in her last days," Manson began, "was sick." The room, which was already dead silent, grew somehow even more still. "She suffered from dementia. I was there, every day, by her side." Manson's fists were clenched at either side of the podium. His knuckles were white, and his face was flushed. "But it wasn't me she wanted." Manson looked at Dan. "It was you." He peered over the small audience. "She didn't call for me in her last days. She called for my brother."

The whole room was frozen. No one moved or even breathed.

"I played the part of my brother. For nearly three years, I let her think I was him. What else was I supposed to do? Deny a dying old woman her one wish?" Manson once again turned toward his brother. "You weren't there for her. But I was. I want you to remember that."

Manson stormed away from the podium. Dan watched helplessly as his brother walked past the transfixed audience and out of the room.

The ending is always the worst,
the last page turned,
A smile deferred.
The bitter longing for more.
But there is no more,
No settling the score.
There is only the end.
Just
the end.

—Mindy

SEVENTEEN

The house bustled with energy. Underage kids held red Solo cups as they chattered drunkenly over music that blared throughout the three-story house. Dan drunkenly descended the staircase, zipping up his pants. His feet carefully bumbled down each step, using the railing for support.

"Bro!" Roger ran up, slopping beer onto the carpet. "Did you bang her?"

"No, we went up there to talk about our feelings, numb-nuts." Dan rubbed his unfocused eyes.

"Guys!" Roger shouted loudly, raising his hands in the air and spilling even more beer. "Dan fucked Rachel!"

Cheering erupted, the music fading behind the mass of noise.

"Seriously, Roger?" Mark approached, less intoxicated than the rest.

"I'm just congratulating our friend." Roger patted Dan's shoulder triumphantly, as if Dan's victory was his own.

Mark pushed Roger into the crowd. "Fuck off." He turned to Dan, asking, "You want some fresh air, man?"

"I could go for a smoke." Dan slurred the words as they headed for the door.

The porch looked out on a large lawn that led to a padlocked gate. Mark handed Dan a smoke. "So how was it? I know you've wanted to bang her since freshman year."

"It was worth the wait." Dan lit the cigarette, inhaling deeply. "Thanks for making it happen."

"I didn't do much; just pushed you in the right direction. Consider it a final gift before you head out for the military."

"Cheers to that." They knocked their red Solo cups together and took long swigs. "What's next for you?"

Mark sighed. "College. My parents were adamant on that."

"Have you chosen a major?"

Mark shook his head. "My dad wants me to choose economics, but I'm thinking social work or education."

"A lot of money in economics." Dan belched loudly while crushing his red Solo cup.

"Money isn't everything," Mark said as he stared into space. "Fuck that white-picket-fence lifestyle."

"Yeah," Dan said as he stood up, preparing to piss from the porch. "Fuck it."

Manson had nowhere to hide now. The shack was gone, and he could stay at Mindy's for only so long. He was stuck inside the walls of that tiny trailer. He sat on the couch, stewing in his misery. He waited for his family to come home, dreading the inevitable confrontation.

His mother walked in alone. Manson waited for Dan to storm in after her, but he was nowhere to be seen. His mother sat down and pulled out a cigarette. She didn't even bother changing out of her funeral clothes. Manson waited for her to say something, but she simply turned on the TV and stared at it blankly.

"Where's Dan?"

"He went to the bar."

Manson waited for her to say something about the funeral. He *wanted* her to say something. Anger boiled in him as he watched her stew in smoke. She breathed in and exhaled, as if wishing for death to take her from her fleshy shell. It was a form of slow suicide she partook in with delight.

"Your mom died." Tears welled up in Manson's eyes as he glared at his mother. A surge of emotion overtook him. "Do you even care?"

She simply continued smoking. Her silence only stoked the fire within Manson.

"How does it feel to know you're a failure?" Manson scowled through the white wisps that infected the air. "You failed both your sons. You never raised us. Grandma had to pick up your slack. You were a shitty mom, a shitty daughter, you couldn't keep a man around—" Manson stopped as his mother turned toward him.

"I could have been someone, you know," she said. She wasn't looking at him; she was looking into her past. "I was homecoming queen all four years of high school. Everyone loved me. I was the star cheerleader, an A student. They told me I was destined for great things." She took a long drag. "But instead, I had you and your brother." Smoke drifted out her mouth as she spoke. She didn't bother blowing it away. She liked the way it rested in the air. "I got knocked up by one of the football players. I don't even remember which one. It wasn't anything special. But in that one moment ... I gave up everything I could have been." She turned back to the TV.

Manson searched for words but only found silence. He leaned back into the couch, stewing in the misery his mom knew all too well. They both wallowed in resentment, not only for one another but for a world they believed they did not control.

Dan was deep in contemplation. He sat at the bar, drink in hand. The red and blue lights of the decrepit building shined at him sadly. Elderly men surrounded him, talking about days they were desperate to relive. Some younger men played pool as classic rock played softly in the background. Dan ignored the ruckus of the room as he relived the day over and over. His brother's words ricocheted inside his skull, echoing endlessly in his mind.

"You weren't there for her. But I was. I want you to remember that."

"Want me to pour you some more?" the bartender asked.

Dan was drawn back into the present moment. "Naw." He pushed away the empty cup. "I've had enough."

"Never heard you say that before," said a voice from behind him. Dan turned to see a slightly overweight man with a cheerless smile, a greasy complexion, and long, oily hair that curled unevenly. "If I remember correctly, your nickname in school was Dan the Drinking Man. You could down more than any of us."

"Roger?" Dan asked as he stood up.

"How are you doing, my man?" Roger held out his fist. Dan lazily bumped it. "I didn't know you were back in town."

"Just for a little while." Dan swayed a little on his feet.

"How have things been? You look fit as fuck. The military treating you well?"

Dan shrugged. "You know … it's a living."

"Got ya there." Roger's crooked teeth made his smile look jagged. "I'm a plumber now. Make damn good money too."

Dan nodded, uninterested. "Uh-huh."

"Pour this man another drink!" Roger shouted to the bartender and then turned to Dan. "Up for a game of pool?"

Dan reluctantly gave in. He thought it might work as a distraction. But all he thought about was home. The more he drank, the more Manson's words infected his mind. *"You weren't there for her ..."*

All the while, Roger droned on about his life—his three wives, his two divorces, his shit kids ...

"I don't regret it," Dan drunkenly blurted as he sent balls flying across the pool table.

"Regret what?" Roger positioned himself for a shot.

"Leaving this shit town."

Roger missed his shot. "Damn it!" He leaned his pool stick against the table. "I don't blame ya. It's a shithole. But at least it's *my* shithole."

Dan scoffed. "I'm glad I didn't end up stuck in a shit life like yours." He stumbled backward, dropping his pool cue.

"You're very drunk," Roger said, trying not to be angry. "You should go home."

"Just imagine," Dan said, ignoring Roger's comment, "if I had stayed here with a dying old woman and a shit brother for company. I would be just like you. I would be at this bar every fucking night just to escape my shit life."

"Hey man, fuck you!" Roger shouted. "You don't fucking know me! You don't know my life!"

"I know you're a fat fuck who can't keep a woman."

Roger came at Dan, swinging his pool cue dramatically. Dan ducked, and it hit the wall. Using Roger's momentum, Dan smashed Roger's face into the pool table, snapping his nose. Blood spewed into the air as Roger fell backward, unconscious.

Dan heard people shouting as he left, but he didn't care. He stumbled outside and down the road. Manson's words continued to echo through his thoughts, filling him with rage at each repetition. He found his way into the trailer park, stumbled up the familiar porch steps, and busted the front door open. Manson and his mother jumped at the sudden entrance.

"You!" Dan pointed at his little brother. "You little shit."

Manson tensed up and jumped off the couch.

"I don't regret it." Dan swayed in his spot. "I don't regret any of it."

His mother took a drag from her cigarette. "Dan, you're drunk."

"Shut the fuck up."

She inhaled the smoke too quickly and coughed in surprise.

"Don't give me that shit," Dan growled. "You never raised us; you never gave a shit. It was always Grandma. And what did she get?" Dan directed his drunken rage at Manson. "She got this little shit!"

"At least I was here for her!" Adrenaline flowed through Manson's veins. He was ready for this. "Where the hell were you when she was dying!"

"Living my fucking life!" Dan stumbled forward a bit, only to sway back. "I'm the only one who's fucking doing that! You're all stuck in this hellhole!"

"At least I care! You say Grandma raised us, but you didn't give enough of a shit to stay with her as she died!"

Their mother cried silently as the brothers shouted at each other.

"Maybe you're right," Dan spat out. "Maybe I don't give a shit. Maybe I'm a prick who ran away from his problems. But you know what? I don't regret it. At least I was able to live my fucking life. I wasn't getting trapped with a dying old woman and a—"

Manson knocked Dan into the TV, shattering the screen. Their mother screamed as they both fell to the floor, covered in glass. Manson sat on top of Dan, his hands wrapped firmly around his brother's throat. His face looked crazed and was red with rage. Dan kicked him in the groin violently. Manson grimaced in pain and fell backward onto the floor.

Dan jumped to his feet, and Manson followed. They were both bloody from cuts but neither seemed fazed. Dan went in for a punch, knocking his brother into the wall. He swung again, but Manson ducked. Dan's hand broke violently through the drywall. Manson hit back, aiming for Dan's stomach. His knuckles dug into flesh forcing vomit to erupt from Dan's mouth. Manson's shirt was soaked in puke. Dan stumbled backward, dragging his hand out of the wall. He blacked out and hit the ground hard.

Manson stood over his brother, breathing heavily. His mother sat in shock. Manson felt someone else in the room. He looked up at the still-open door. A large black woman stood there, her cheeks stained with tears.

"Felicia?" Manson said.

Mindy's mom had a single piece of paper in her hand. "Manson." Her voice was a whisper. She was looking down at Dan. "Now's not a good time ..." Her voice was distant and detached.

"Why are you ..." Manson couldn't find the rest of the sentence as he stepped toward her.

"I would have told you earlier if I could have."

Manson took the paper from Felicia's hand. He looked at it blankly, not understanding at first. His heart dropped into his stomach, and dread consumed him. The words written across the top said it all: *Suicide Note*.

I am the empty girl,
The girl with a thousand faces.
But none of them are mine.
I am just a stain,
Driven into the carpet,
Left to fade away.
I'll fade away.
And let others dance in the remains.

—Mindy

EIGHTEEN

There was something calming about him. His presence made Mindy feel at ease. She ran her fingers through his long hair as they lay naked on the green couch. The heat of the day had caused them to shed their clothing and lay motionless, having nothing better to do than be in each other's company.

"You work today?" Manson asked as he knocked his cigarette against a makeshift ashtray.

"Naw." Mindy snuggled closer to him, her eyes fixed on some unknown point. "You?"

"Nope. You want to do something?"

"Like what?"

"I don't know." Sweat dripped from Manson's brow despite the warm breeze that cascaded in through the open door. "Lake Michigan isn't far."

"You going to bike there?"

"Good one." Manson pressed the butt of his cigarette against the wall, extinguishing it.

"Oh, cool," Dex blurted as he walked in. "We're a nudist colony now. How quaint."

"You want to go to Lake Michigan?" Mindy asked as she stood up, stretching.

Dex looked away. "Jesus Christ! I don't want to see that shit! Put some fucking clothes on!"

"Only if you'll say you'll go."

"Fine, whatever. Anything to hide my eyes from that shit."

"I like it," Manson said, flicking his cigarette at Dex. Mindy laughed.

After an hour-long car ride, the trio ascended a large dune with Dex in the lead. Mindy's fingers filled the spaces between Manson's knuckles. *Strange*, she thought, *how human hands were meant for holding; how one's fingers fit perfectly between another's.*

"I'm king of the world!" Dex yelled dramatically, flinging his arms out, as they reached the top of the dune. He looked at the other two. "*Titanic?*"

"This is why no one was surprised to learn you are gay," Manson jested.

"Fuck off." Dex lowered his arms. "Race you to the bottom?"

"We're going to take a breather," Mindy said as she plopped down onto the sand. "You go ahead. We'll meet you down there in a bit."

"Suit yourself, losers." Dex ran down the hill, making it halfway before falling and rolling head over heels onto the beach.

Mindy laughed. "He's a character."

"Yeah." Manson looked at his girlfriend, admiring how the sun hit her sculpted cheeks perfectly. Her hair blew gently in the warm breeze as their joined hands lay in the sand. Manson suddenly had a vision of them sixty years from now, their skin wrinkled and their eyes heavy with the burden of age. But their hands were still entwined, laying peacefully on the sand. Their bodies had grown old, but their souls were still as fresh as the day they'd first met.

Mindy chuckled, noticing Manson's persistent gaze. "What?"

He smiled and leaned in to kiss her. Their lips met, and Manson wished that moment would stretch into forever. "Come on," he whispered. "Race you to the bottom."

There was a profound emptiness inside her that could not be described with mere words. She had tried many times. The pages of her journal were scrawled with poems and passages trying to do just that. She sometimes described it as a gnawing. At other times, it was an aching. At its worst, it was a nothingness. The *nothing* was what scared her the most.

> *Nothingness* is a profound word. The concept of nothing in itself cannot be explained. For who knows what nothing is? You can't touch nothing, you can't breathe nothing, you can't be nothing, you can't see nothing … but you can feel nothing. I can. It's like a blank space encompassing my insides. Like a black hole sucking away every emotion. Like …

Mindy scribbled over what she had written and threw down her pen. She pushed the journal aside. She turned over and stared at the ceiling. Not even words could help her escape the prison that grew from her soul and encircled her mind. The dullness inside her grew, its black fingers reaching into every thought with malice.

Her thoughts wandered to the image of Manson. She wanted his smile to infect her; she wanted his eyes to drag her from this all-too-familiar pit. But the image of him was like an old photograph that had rotted on an ancient wall. It felt like an old memory she would look back on with remorse and regret.

She wished he was here. She would be happy then. But it would be a false happiness. A happiness that would leave with him. No, it wouldn't leave with him. She would be the one who left it behind. After all, she was the one who was leaving for college, not him.

Mindy sighed. She promised herself every night that she would not reach beneath her bed, that she would not grab the dark secret that lay there. This was one of those nights she would break that promise, and it would break her.

She leaned over the edge of the bed and reached beneath her, feeling around until she found the box. She pulled it out, the wood cold against her fingers. She placed it on the bed and stared at it. She tried convincing herself not to open it, but it was no use. She lifted the top off and placed it next to her pillow. The box was full of small slips of rolled-up paper. One by one, she read them. They all had the same header: *Suicide Note.*

Some of them were similar, but all of them were different. The scrawled words changed tone, depending on what shape Mindy's mind had contorted into. Some sounded desperate, others angry. They all had an underlying sadness running through their blotchy ink—a sadness and a guilt that was rooted in the mess she was sure to leave behind.

That's what always stopped her. The guilt. She couldn't leave, knowing the ruin she would leave in her wake. The pain she'd cause her family, the sadness she'd inflict on her friends, and the confusion she'd leave Manson in. Her life wasn't hers. Everyone owned a piece of it. It's what kept her going.

But tonight she was being selfish. The dullness was eating at her, chipping away at the parts of her soul that still lingered. She had to remind herself that it wasn't always like this. She didn't always feel this way. The days were better; she could distance herself from these feelings. But the nights ... As she had once written, "it's hard to hide from yourself when you're the only one in the room."

She tried to fight the urge but nonetheless found a fresh piece of paper in front of her. Before she knew it, *Suicide Note* was scrawled at the top. But this time it felt different. It felt like a final draft. She went to her desk and found scissors. She cut off sections of each note and glued them to the new one. It was a papier-mâché death note.

It seemed to take hours to fill the page. She strategically placed each word. With painstaking thought, she contemplated each phrase, each sentence; every thought had to be perfect. But it never would be. It would always be unfinished and imperfect in some way.

The minutes ticked into hours, and Mindy began to accept that it would never be perfect. No matter how meticulously she constructed the sentences or how much detail she put into every word, her feelings would not translate. Others would read it and feel what they felt, not what she felt. Tears welled in her eyes, and a bitter despair echoed through the chasm in her chest.

She ripped the paper to shreds. She grabbed a fresh paper and scrawled two simple words beneath the familiar header. Afterward, she dug her head into a pillow, trying not to breathe. She didn't have to do this. She didn't have to be this. But she was. No matter how much she tried not to be this, it is what she was. She scrawled one last poem in her journal.

I am the empty girl,
The girl with a thousand faces.
But none of them are mine.

I am just a stain,
Driven into the carpet,
Left to fade away.
I'll fade away,
And let others dance in the remains.

She pushed the journal aside and pressed her hands into her wet eyes. The insignificance of existence ate at her and clouded her mind with profound grief. Before she knew what she was doing, she had a blade in her hand. It scraped down the length of her arm. The pain brought relief with it. Just for a moment, the aching subsided. Mindy exhaled, caught in the ecstasy of pain.

But the moment passed, like all moments do. And suddenly, blood was soaking into the sheets like it never had before. Waves of ruby-red jewels dripped down her arm. In a moment of illogical panic, she tried shoving the blood back into her arm. But all that resulted in more blood splattering onto her. She looked longingly at her bloody palm, realizing that there was no turning back.

Each heartbeat grew fainter. Mindy lost track of where the bed began and where the blood started. She grew woozy. It occurred to her that she would never see her family again. She would never feel Manson's lips again. She realized, in that moment, that all her problems were solvable, except the one she had just created.

She died feeling regret.

NINETEEN

"Do you think God exists?" Mindy asked. They were sitting on the edge of the cliff, staring across the forest. The setting sun cast shadows over the pristine landscape.

"No," Manson answered honestly.

"Why?"

"I've never seen him."

Mindy swung her legs back and forth, her heels hitting the rock face forcefully. "You can go your entire life without seeing something. Doesn't mean it doesn't exist."

"I just don't believe in stuff like that."

"I think it's a nice idea." Mindy rubbed against Manson. She always liked to be as close to him as possible. "I like to think that there's something better after this."

"It *is* a nice idea; it's just hard for me to buy. This is it. If we screw this up, there's no second chance."

"Well, that's reassuring." She'd said it sarcastically, but the thought haunted her.

Manson pedaled furiously. Tears infested his eyes. They flowed off his cheeks and stained the road beneath his wheels. His heart pounded with the beat of grief and confusion. His white knuckles gripped the handlebars, a crumpled note held haphazardly in them. His legs burned, but he didn't care.

His mind was clogged with thoughts. He unconsciously directed himself back to the shack. Or at least what was left of it. He let the bike fall to the ground as he collapsed next to a tree. He shook uncontrollably as tears stained the suicide note. He read the two words over and over.

I'm sorry.

He tried sifting through the confusion to find some explanation. The phrase burned into his mind like hot coals.

"You didn't have to be," Manson whispered. "You didn't have to be sorry."

He saw the bags of alcohol that Dex had left behind. They sat there as if waiting for Manson's inevitable return. He reached into them and began drowning his sorrow in liquor. As he drank, he read the note over and over.

I'm sorry.

I'm sorry.

I'm sorry.

"You didn't have to be."

I'm sorry.

I'm sorry.

I'm sorry.

"You didn't have to be ..." The words kept slipping off Manson's tongue.

I'm sorry.

I'm sorry.

I'm sorry.

"You didn't have to be!" Manson shouted and threw the bottle. It shattered as it hit the car. Shards of glass sprinkled onto the ground. Manson stumbled to his feet and found his way to the ashy remains.

He walked through the rubble, a graveyard of memories flooding his mind. Getting high with Dex, sleeping on that green couch ... but mainly, he remembered Mindy. Her smile, her quips, her long black locks, her body entwined with his ... those memories were all tainted now. Tainted by despair and a feeling of unfinishedness.

In all the time they had spent together, had she known? *Had she planned this?* Manson wondered. Every time the words *I love you* spilled from her lips, did she know the pain she would inflict? Was this her plan all along? Or was it worse—did she just not care? Did she not think of him in her final moments?

Manson wandered past what was left of the couch. That was the first place they had made love. The memory pounded inside him, sending pain reverberating through every bone in his body. He leaned over and vomited. It splattered against the scorched ground and spread itself around his feet.

He wandered over to the shattered bottle. The neck had stayed intact. He picked it up, the shattered end gleaming in the light. That's how she must have done it. She must have cut herself. Manson envisioned the glass scraping over his wrists, the blood dripping quickly onto the cold, hard ground. In that moment, he understood Mindy's pain.

I'm sorry.

"No, you're not."

Manson stumbled into the forest, leaving the wreckage behind.

"Her funeral is today."

They were sitting outside Mindy's apartment. Their legs hung in the air as they leaned against the railing. They gazed blankly at the dark parking lot. The street lights cast their glow over the bleak night. Not a soul was in sight.

"How do you feel about that?" Mindy asked.

"Fine, I guess."

"That's a lie."

"I know," Manson admitted, "but saying it makes me feel better."

Mindy slipped her hand into his. "It's okay."

"I'm scared."

"Of what?" Mindy asked.

"The future." He wrapped his fingers tightly around her knuckles. "What's going to happen to us when you go to college?"

"I don't know."

The honesty of the conversation frightened them both. They stared into the darkness together, as if waiting for the night to end.

TWENTY

They were huddled around a small fire. Their guns were pointed down at the sandy ground. Nights in Iraq weren't as hot as the days, but they still weren't pleasant, especially when weighed down by military-grade apparel.

"I'd die for some good pussy right now." It was Sam. He was always overly crude.

"Well, you shouldn't have signed up for a sausage fest, numb-nuts." Thad didn't put up with Sam's shit.

"You two sound like a bickering couple." Dan this time. He looked longingly at the dancing flames in front of him.

"I'm just saying, dude, I miss waking up with a girl next to me. Morning pussy is the best pussy."

"You talk so much about pussy I'm starting to think you're gay."

"You wish, Thad."

"No, thanks. My husband is a better man than you'll ever be."

"What about you, Dan?" Sam asked. "You got anyone special?"

"I got my family." Dan continued to gaze at the fire. "That's about it."

"No high school sweetheart?" I had this time.

"Naw, I didn't have the time, considering ..." Dan stopped himself.

"Considering what?" Sam asked.

"I just didn't have time. I had to take care of my brother. My mom was a deadbeat. My grandma did what she could, but by the time I left, she was getting too old."

"Damn, dude ... I'm sorry."

"Don't be." Dan shifted, moving the dirt beneath him. "We all have shit in our past. No big deal."

"How's your brother doing?" Thad asked.

"I don't know. I haven't talked to him since ... since I left."

"No calls home? Why?"

"Not many. It's just ... been so long. I don't know what I'd say."

"You sound like a fucking coward."

Dan looked up. Thad had transformed into Manson. His long hair reflected the glowing firelight, and his hands held his long legs close to his chest.

"This is a dream, isn't it?"

The pounding headache hit Dan before he even opened his eyes. It was like a pulsating worm digging deeper and deeper into his skull. He lay motionless for the better part of an hour before slowly peeling his eyes open. He groaned and sat up.

He wasn't sure how he got there, but he was on his grandmother's bed. The sheets still smelled like her, and the fan still swung lazily overhead like it always had. Dan felt a strange sensation overcome him. It was a sad nostalgia. Vague memories of his grandmother filled his mind. The smell of her cookies, her old, crackly voice calling his name … it all seemed so familiar yet alien.

Dan worked his way into the living room, wincing at the pounding headache. His mom was on the carpeted floor with a sponge and a bucket of steaming-hot water. She didn't look up at him as her arms methodically scrubbed the floor.

"What happened?" Dan asked, his voice craggy.

"You were drunk."

"I guessed that from the headache." He waited for a more in-depth explanation, but his mom only gazed at the floor. "What are you cleaning?" Dan asked.

"Your vomit."

Dan rubbed his hands through his short hair. "I'm sorry." Again he waited for a response, and again, he did not get one. "Where's Manson?"

"He ran away." Her voice was heavy.

"What do you mean he ran away?"

She stopped scrubbing for just a moment. She looked up, her eyes burdened. "His girlfriend … she killed herself."

Dan had difficulty processing the information. The words bounced around in his skull. "The little black girl … she's dead?"

"Her mom stopped by and told Manson. He ran away, and she left."

"You let him leave!" Dan shouted.

"I couldn't stop him." She continued scrubbing the floor.

"I doubt you tried." Dan bitterly retorted as he headed for the door.

"I wouldn't go after him if I were you."

Dan stopped halfway out the door.

"You and Manson got in a fight while you were drunk ..."

"He's my fucking brother." Dan continued out the door. "I'm going to find him."

Dan didn't close the door; he left his mother to do it for him.

INTERLUDE

"Honey?" Felicia knocked on the door. The smell of eggs and freshly buttered toast filled the apartment. "Honey?" She knocked harder this time. "Time to get up! You have to be to work in an hour." She entered the room, flipping the lights on. "Did you not set an alarm—"

Felicia suddenly screamed. The bed was stained a deep red, and Mindy's wrists were broken open, her insides dry to the bone. Felicia ran over, propping Mindy's head in her arms. Felicia pushed Mindy's hair behind her ear, looking into the lifeless eyes that used to gleam with youthfulness.

"What the hell—" Richard bounded in but stopped dead in his tracks. "Oh my God ..."

"Call an ambulance!" Felicia pleaded, clutching Mindy's cold hands. "We can still save her. There's still time!"

"Daddy?" Thomas came down the hallway.

"No!" Richard shouted, scooping up his son. "Let's go into your room. You can bring the Xbox but only if you promise to stay put."

"Cool!" Thomas shouted, unaware of the grief that permeated the apartment.

A short while later, medics showed up carrying a body bag.

"What's that?" Felicia asked, still holding her daughter's motionless body.

"I'm sorry, ma'am," one of the medics said softly. "We need to take her before the body starts—"

"You have to save her!" Felicia shouted. "You have to save her!"

"Ma'am …"

"I won't let you take her!" Felicia clutched the body close to her. "You have to save her! You have to!"

"Felicia," Richard said, his voice heavy, "let the men take her."

"No … no, we have to save her!"

"She's dead, Felicia." Richard grabbed his wife, pulling her away from the corpse.

"No," Felicia said weakly, falling to the floor. "No, no, no …" Tears streamed from her eyes as the men carefully placed the body in the bag. "No!" The scream was full of grief so profound it seemed to taint the air around it. "No! Not my baby!"

Richard held his wife as the men walked out.

Felicia sat on the bed, her hands moving across the dried blood. Despite the carnage, the room still smelled like Mindy. Her posters still hung on the walls, and the pink esthetic still popped out like a frame from a storybook.

"Honey." It was Richard. "It's been a week. We need—"

"I know," Felicia whispered. "I know."

They took the sheets off and dragged the mattress out of the apartment. A few neighbors watched as they lugged the mattress into the dumpster. They'd all heard the wails a week earlier and had seen the body bag.

Felicia gazed at the mattress. It was strange, but the blood made Felicia feel as if she had some lingering connection to her daughter. And now, that was gone. The small piece of her daughter that had still lived with them now lay among rubble.

Richard slammed the dumpster shut. "Come on." He grabbed his wife's hand. "It's time to tell Junior the truth."

TWENTY ONE

Dan drove to the shack first. All he found were burned remains and empty beer bottles. He checked the gas station and even asked the manager if he had seen Manson. He swept the town twice over, looking for any sign of his brother.

The day dragged on until it could drag on no longer, and evening crept over the decrepit town. Dan became more and more panicked. He looked in every nook and cranny, even asking strangers if they'd seen a tall, gangly boy. Then, as the sun set, it hit him. *The railroad tracks.* He couldn't believe he hadn't thought to check there.

Dan sped to the familiar location. He pulled over, parking on the side of the road. His headlights fell on a bike leaning against the trees. The pink sky loomed overhead as Dan jogged down the tracks.

"Manson!" He shouted his brother's name as he ran. His voice bounced back at him.

"Manson!" Dan found the familiar path through the woods. He galloped through the thick vegetation, the twigs and leaves nipping at his heels. "Manson!" Dan burst through onto the cliff face.

Manson sat, his feet dangling. He held a shattered bottle. His eyes were glazed over with tears. Dan approached slowly.

"Why are you here?" Manson's voice was harsh and bitter. He still clung to the suicide note. The edges that weren't held in his tight grip shook in the light breeze.

"I came to get you. I want to make sure you're okay."

"You shouldn't have come." Manson loosened his grip and let the note blow away. It drifted downward, eventually landing among the trees.

"What was that?"

Manson's lip quivered. "Her suicide note."

"Manson … I'm sorry."

"Spare me your pity." Manson gripped the bottle tightly. "Last time I saw you, you called me a little shit. Don't start acting like you give one now."

"Whatever I said while I was drunk, I'm sorry." Dan's voice was desperate and thick with emotion. "I understand you want nothing to do with me … but I'm your brother. I know I can be an asshole, but I care about you. I love you. And I want to make sure—"

"Look at them." Manson abruptly interrupted Dan's monologue. "All those people." Manson pointed at the distant town, its silhouette fading in the dark. "They all live their lives with such self-importance. They don't care that Mindy died. They won't care when I die. And I won't care when they die."

"Manson … I understand you're grieving. But come home with me. We can talk there."

Manson ignored his brother. "It all seems so pointless, doesn't it?" He looked blankly at a sky that was fading from pink to a blueish-black. "They're like flies buzzing about, so frantic. And yet their existence is so pointless."

"Listen ... I'm sorry about what happened to Mindy. Let's talk about this at—"

"You didn't even know her," Manson snapped.

"You're right. I didn't. But I can tell how much she meant to you. Whenever you were gone, I knew you were with her. And you were gone a lot."

Manson looked away. "It doesn't matter. She's gone now."

"Of course it matters!" Dan said desperately. "All those times you had with her ... just because she's gone doesn't mean they didn't happen. The same with Grandma, or anyone else who dies. You will always have those memories."

"Why should I listen to you?" Manson's eyes shifted as he himself looked for a reason.

"Because I'm right."

"Were you right when you called Mom a shit mother?" Manson bitterly spat out the words. "Were you right when you said you were happy you'd left me with a dying old lady?"

"Manson, I'm sorry"—Dan's calm edge was slipping away—"but that's not what this is about."

"That's what this is all about!" Manson shouted, mad with grief. "If you hadn't left, I would have been able to go to college while living at home. We both could have taken care of Grandma; we both could have lived our lives! But you had to go as far away as you could get." Manson stood up and faced his brother. "If it weren't for you, I could have left this town. I would have never met Mindy; none of this would have happened! She might even still be here."

"Manson ..." Dan looked for the right words. "You're grieving. You're looking for someone to blame. I'm sorry I left you behind. I'm sorry I never called. But Mindy's death ... that's not my fault. Her death was a tragedy."

"You're right." Manson stumbled around, still a bit drunk. "It's not your fault. It's mine."

"No," Dan pleaded. "This is not your fault."

"The cuts on her arms ... the things she told me ... I should have known."

Dan approached his brother, trying to put a comforting hand on his shoulder. Manson lurched back violently, the sharp glass cutting Dan's face as Manson swung his hand upward. Dan fell to the ground, clutching the fresh wound. Blood flowed, dripping into the creases of his fingers. Manson stumbled toward the woods. Dan took his hand away, revealing a large gash from his cheekbone to his lower eye. He let the warm blood curve down his face and drip off his chin.

"I'm ... I'm ..." Manson didn't bother to finish. He ran into the woods, turning his back on his brother and the dark landscape below them.

"Manson!" Dan ran after his brother.

Off in the distance, a train whistle blew.

Night had fully enveloped the forest. Dan blindly tripped his way through the dark, following the sound of his brother's rapid footsteps.

"Manson!" Blood continued gushing out his cheek, the warm fluid slithering down his neck and soaking the collar of his shirt.

Manson scuttered up the steep incline leading to the railroad. By the time he reached the tracks, he was breathing heavily. The sound of an oncoming train pierced the night. Its shrill call echoed through the trees, which blew in a fierce wind. Manson's mop of hair was blown about along with the shadowy leaves.

Manson could sense his brother a few paces behind him. He clenched his jaw tightly, his tear-filled eyes blinking rapidly. Despair, frustration, and anger pounded through him. He tightly clutched the glass, his brother's blood still fresh on the jagged surface.

"Manson, stop running!" Dan's bloody face gleamed in the shadowy moonlight.

"Why do you have to do this?" Manson's voice was rough as he shouted. "Why don't you just go back! Leave! My life was shit before you came back, but at least people weren't dying!"

The train sounded again, a little louder this time. Dan could see it coming in the distance. Its headlight flickered behind the cover of trees.

"Manson …" Dan remained as calm as he could. "We need to leave. If we hurry, we can get back to the car before the train gets here."

"You never said anything to me about the funeral." Manson's back was still turned to his brother.

"Manson!" Dan was losing his composure. The ground was beginning to quiver slightly. "We need to get out of here!"

"What did you expect when you called me up on that stage?" Manson asked.

"I don't know!" Dan shouted in panic. "I don't know what I was thinking! I just didn't know what to say!"

Manson laughed. "So you put the burden on me. Like you always do."

"What do you want from me!" Dan yelled, exasperated. "I'm sorry! I am! But I can't change the past!"

The train had come around the curve in the tracks. The ground shook violently. Dark smoke mixed with the black night. The oncoming light glowed against Dan's wet cheek. Manson's shadow extended as the train approached.

"We need to get off these tracks!"

"Why?" Manson smiled manically. He bathed in the majesty of his oncoming doom. "The people I care about are dead. Why shouldn't I join them?"

"Because you are so much more than them!" Dan let all caution go. "You have so much more life to live! I know you're hurting. I know you can't see a future, but you have one!" Dan was choking up now. Tears mingled with the blood below his eyes. "I have seen things, Manson. I have done things in the military ... I have saved people, and I have killed others. I've had the worst days of my life and the best. Life is so much more than one moment. It's so much more than what you're feeling right now. You'll survive this, and you'll see better days."

Manson chose not to hear his brother. The train was close now. He looked into the light, like a moth being drawn to a flame. The faces of those he'd lost, those he'd never see again, flew by. Mindy, Dex, his grandma ... they were no more than haunting memories now. He blocked them out, refusing to feel the flood of emotion. He would never have to feel again after this. He wanted that desperately.

"Manson!"

Dan's voice was drowned out by the thundering roar of the train. It sped forward, a monolith of oncoming death. Dan ran toward his brother and spun him around. Manson lashed out, digging the shattered bottle into his brother's stomach. Dan winced in pain. Manson drove the bottle deeper into his brother's flesh. He had been driven mad by the sadness.

Dan looked his brother in the eyes, a pained expression on his face. Manson looked back. A stillness suddenly overtook the moment. A profound calm overcame them both. They looked at one another in a way they hadn't since they were kids.

"I love you, brother." Dan said the words quietly, but Manson heard him. The train overcame them.

TWENTY TWO

Manson awoke to the smell of his grandmother's cooking. She was making pancakes. That meant it was Saturday. He jumped out of bed, his small feet trotting to his brother's side.

"Wake up!" He shook his brother, who hid beneath sheets. "It's Saturday. Grandma made pancakes."

Dan rolled over lazily. "I want to sleep in."

"It's ten, you lazybones." Manson smiled, revealing a lack of teeth. New ones were beginning to grow out of the gaps his old ones had left behind.

Dan groaned and rolled over, covering his head in blankets.

"Grandma won't be happy." Manson leaped happily out of the room, his bare feet slapping against the floor.

The threat of Grandma's unhappiness forced Dan to his feet. He trudged out of the room.

In the kitchen, Grandma was busy at the stove. She wore a flowery dress, and her hair was held up in a tight bun. Her daughter sat in front of the TV. She pulled out a pack of cigarettes and looked at them longingly.

"Not in the house." Grandma's voice was stern but not without its loving edge.

"I'll go outside, then." Her daughter stood up and headed for the door.

"I grabbed you an application from the gas station." Grandma gently flipped over a pancake. "I want you to fill it out today."

"I'll do it later." She reached for her lighter as she walked out the door.

"Why not now?"

"Because I need a smoke."

"You need to start pulling your own weight." The loving edge was fading from Grandma's voice. "You've been unemployed for more than a month. I won't be around forever, you know. Someone's got to take care of these kids."

It was no use. Her daughter was already out the door.

"Grandma!" Manson hugged his grandma's leg. "Are the pancakes ready?"

"Almost."

Dan trudged in lazily.

A short while later, they all sat at the table. Manson gulped down pancakes while his brother neatly cut his.

"Manson, slow down."

"Sorry," he said with a full mouth. Syrup dripped down his chin. His grandma wiped it away with a napkin.

"Try to eat like your brother. See how he cuts his pancake with his fork? Do that next time instead of shoveling the whole thing into your mouth."

Dan looked proud as he neatly dipped his pancake wedges in syrup.

"After breakfast you're going to take your brother for a walk." The comment was directed at Dan.

He groaned. "Do I have to?"

"You always have fun. Don't act like you don't. Besides, I don't want you two sitting around the house all day. You can spend two hours going for a walk, and then you can watch an hour of television. Agreed?"

"Agreed." Dan and Manson said in unison.

After breakfast they stopped by the gas station to get sodas. Dan paid in quarters. "Where do you want to go?" He sipped on his drink as they walked across the parking lot. The carbonation burned his throat in a pleasant way.

"The cliff!" Manson bounced around.

"We always go there."

"It's so cool!"

They took the long walk down the tracks and to the cliff. They let their legs hang over the edge. The sun beat down on their backs, and sweat slithered down their brows. Neither of them seemed to mind as they overlooked the deep green forest and the distant town.

"If Grandma knew we came here, she'd kill us." Manson had already chugged his soda. "She'd say it's dangerous."

"Never tell her." Dan's voice was as serious as a nine-year-old's could be. "I don't want to get in trouble."

Manson threw his soda can over the edge of the cliff.

"Why'd you do that?" Dan exclaimed. "That's littering!"

"I wanted to see it fall."

"That's weird."

"You're weird." Manson pushed his brother playfully.

"Don't do that, dummy! We're on a cliff!"

"What if we both fell down and died?" Manson posed the hypothetical in an all-too-happy voice.

"Grandma would be angry."

They both laughed. Even at their age, they realized the absurdity of that statement.

"I hope I live as long as Grandma," Manson blurted, "Maybe even longer."

"I hope I die in combat." Dan formed his hand into a pistol and closed his left eye to aim more accurately. He made shooting sounds as he aimed at the world below him.

"You still want to be a soldier?"

"Yeah."

"Dan, the soldier man."

"I told you not to call me that."

"I know you still play with our old army men."

"Do not!"

"Do to!"

Dan shoved his brother, less playfully than Manson had pushed him. Manson laughed, knowing that he had won the conversation.

"I want to be an archaeologist." Manson's toothless grin showed his wonder.

"What's that?"

"Scientists who dig up dinosaur bones. I read about it in a book."

"Books are for losers."

"You're just saying that because I read better than you."

Dan chose not to respond. "Come on. I want to watch TV."

"It hasn't been two hours," Manson protested as they both stood up.

"It will be by the time we get home."

The pair walked back down the tracks.

"What are you writing?" Manson took a drag as he looked down at Mindy. They were outside the shack in the old car.

"A book." Her nose was buried deep in a notebook. She scrawled furiously.

"I thought you didn't write books."

"I never finish them. I just start them."

"Why start something you know you won't finish?"

They could hear Dex coughing in the shack. Smoke wafted out from beneath the closed door.

Mindy shrugged, tossing her head back and pausing for a moment. "I want to finish one someday. I'm just really bad at endings."

"Why?"

"I can never think of a happy one."

"Why does the ending have to be happy?" Manson's voice was wheezy as smoke sprang from his mouth.

"It doesn't. I just want it to be."

Manson's brow furrowed in confusion. "Then ... why not just end it with 'They lived happily ever after. The end'?"

"It's not that easy."

"I think you're just a pessimist." The trees blew gently.

"Maybe." Mindy paused for a moment. "It's just that ... good endings should have a point. What point does a happy ending have?"

Manson laughed. "To make people happy."

"I guess that's the thing. I have a hard time with happy endings because all the endings I've seen aren't happy."

"You're confusing me."

They heard Dex coughing again.

"Well ... think about it," she said. "When things end in the real world, are you happy about it?"

"Depends what's ending."

They heard Dex yell, "That's some good shit!"

They both chose to ignore him.

Mindy sighed. "Things don't end in the real world. They either keep going, or they change and then keep going. The only real ending in life is death."

"I think I hit it on the head when I called you a pessimist."

Mindy's eyes suddenly became sad. "I never said you were wrong."

EPILOGUE

The old man wandered through the graveyard. A light wind blew as he stroked his short beard. The leafy canopy shifted endlessly, rays of light dancing with the motion. He wandered far, passing grave after grave. The farther he went, the more unkempt the graves became. It was as the man had realized years ago—everything succumbs to time and everything is forgotten.

The man found the grave he was looking for. He sighed, crouching down. He placed a bouquet of flowers beneath the headstone. A pile of rotted roses sat there. It looked like someone had been placing them there for years.

"I have a lot to regret." The man stroked his beard therapeutically. The white whiskers rustled against his fingers lightly. "But the thing I regret most is leaving. I don't know how much I could have changed, but if I'd been here when you died, I might ... I might ..."

Tears welled up in his eyes. He felt a stab of pain in his chest. Exhaling, he closed his eyes, trying to prevent the tears. They came anyway.

The warm wind blew dead vegetation over the graves. The old man looked around. He was almost angry that the weather was pleasant. He wanted it to be gloomy to match his mood.

"That's the difference between you and me. You chose death while death chose me. The difference between you and me ..." The man paused, clenching his jaw. "You dragged people down with you. That's something I would never do."

The man walked away. He didn't look back. The grave stayed and decayed. The name engraved would one day fade and be forgotten. But for the present moment it read,

Mindy
Beloved daughter and sister

Below that:

I'll fade away
And let others dance in the remains.

Printed in the United States
By Bookmasters